Praise for Kim .

"In *The Strangeness of Men*, Wright displays an uncanny ability to reveal significance in moments of profound mundanity. These pieces, a beautifully orchestrated collection of stories and poems, speak to our human fragility and resilience. Here, even the briefest encounters resonate with startling insight and poignancy." —Rebeca Morales, editor, *The Milo Review*

"Kim Drew Wright's *The Strangeness of Men* traverses an emotional terrain spanning the complications of modern love to the secrets of lives in subdivisions. With a quick eye to popular culture and sympathy for the small, human moments that make a life meaningful, this collection takes the reader on a journey through the extraordinary within the ordinary." —Renée K. Nicholson, editor, *Souvenir*, author of *Roundabout Directions to Lincoln Center*

Praise for "The Long Road" from Sixfold Journal contest readers

"Just finished reading 'The Long Road.' What an amazing story. I don't think I've ever been so angered and so moved at the same time by a short story. Brilliant. Thank you. I haven't been this affected by something I read in a long time." —Rosalyn

"Absolutely wonderful story. This is the only story I've read in this competition in which I truly cared about the main character. I really wanted him to make it to the test and show those jerks that he was more than just a houseboy. Very well done. This was my top pick for the final round of voting." —Mark

"I want more....The writing is descriptive and spare. The people, even in their foreignness, feel universal and real. The geography is as vital as a character. Is this part of a longer piece, a novel or linked stories? I hope it is. I found myself rooting for Billie. I want to know what happens to him." —Shirley

"This is a remarkable story about courage and determination. Very inspiring." —Anonymous

"Absolutely wonderful story, so descriptive. I did not want it to end. In fact, I could have read a whole book." —Sandie

THE STRANGENESS OF MEN

KIM DREW WRIGHT

quickwitlit

Published in the United States by
Quick Wit Lit, L.L.C.
PO Box 4532, Midlothian, VA 23112

First Edition
© 2015 by Kim Drew Wright

Some stories received awards or previously appeared in an edited version by the
following: "How My Day Went" in *Ascent Aspirations* (August 2013), *What We Carry
Home Anthology* (2013), and as "What I Did All Day" in *Everyday Epistle* (October
2012); "Tighter" in Library of Virginia online (July 2013); "Last Chance Nightclub"
as "Reveille" in Library of Virginia online (July 2013); "King of the Heap" in *Circa:
A Journal of Historical Fiction* (October 2013); "Making Space" in *The Milo Review*
(March 2014); "Ain't Nothing but a Chicken Wing" in *The Pinch Journal* (Fall 2014);
"Giraffes" in *Boston Literary Magazine* (Winter 2014–2015); "American Holiday" in
Quick Wit Lit (November 26, 2014), and *Real Spiel* (December 2014); "Burnt Wings,"
Honorable Mention in Writer Unboxed flash fiction contest (January 2015); "How
to Cross the Street Without Dying" in *1000words* (January 2015); "The Long Road"
in *Sixfold Journal*, Fourth Place Fiction Winner (March 2015); "The Ice Swimmer,"
Fourth Place in heat in *NYC Midnight* competition (March 2015); "Dust Therapy,"
Honorable Mention in Poetry Virginia 2015 Edgar Allan Poe Memorial; and "A
Conversation with Andromeda at the Assisted Living Facility," Honorable Mention in
Poetry Virginia 2015 Brodie Herndon Memorial.

Cover design by James T. Egan of Bookfly Design.
Edited by Kira Rubenthaler of Bookfly Design.
Author photo by Jessica Elmendorf Photography.

Library of Congress Control Number: 2015941810
ISBN 978-0-9861964-0-9 print edition
ISBN 978-0-9861964-1-6 epub format
ISBN 978-0-9861964-2-3 mobi format

CONTENTS

Love – a Definition: 3

The Ice Swimmer 5

Technically Related 17

Ain't Nothing but a Chicken Wing 19

Sundaes and Apple Pie 23

Daily Ration 24

Pretty Enough... 30

Wish You Were Here.. 32

Your Voice... 36

Making Space.. 38

Something Found 43

Helluvaguy.. 45

Lessons in Remembering.. 48

Heart's Artillery... 50

How to Cross the Street Without Dying 58

The Long Road 60

Burnt Wings 71

Heart Insurance 73

Giraffes 81

Treading Water.. 83

American Holiday.. 86

Dog Tired 90

Dust Therapy 94

Wonder Woman in Suburbia 95

Andromeda on the Strangeness of Men 97

Andromeda Looks at Fifty.. 98

A Conversation with Andromeda at the Assisted Living Facility........ 100

To-Do List 101

How My Day Went 107

Laundry... 109

Stuck on You... 111

Junk Mail.. 114

Altavista.. 120

Tighter... 125

King of the Heap 129

Last Chance Nightclub 133

Night School Showdown 135

Lighter... 137

Acknowledgments... 141

THE STRANGENESS
OF MEN

Happy reading!
May you discover
adventures in everyday
journeys. Kent

LOVE – A DEFINITION: (NOUN)

1. constant affection for another. 2. tenderness felt by lovers. 3. based on admiration or common interests. 4. warm attachment or devotion. 5. a beloved person: *DARLING*. 6. unselfish, loyal concern for the good of another.

1. He touches my hair, shows he cares by carrying the trash to the curb, heaves a commiserate sigh when I bitch about my friend's liar boyfriend. I believe him when he says he has to work late. After all, he deposits a paycheck monthly, balances work and house, embraces his imperfect *spouse*.

2. I always come first, where he's concerned. He's concerned about my mood swings and if he's shoveled the correct inches of wood chips under the playset. I bet, in the dark recesses of my heart, he'd be happier with another lady, a smidge less crazy, who'd be chipper when he came home. I'd like to lick this habit of putting him down, but a learned lesson *sticks*.

3. We appreciate a hoppy beer, Canadian whiskey on rocks. Tequila shots got us back together after freshman year, when he crushed my heart parading around a short girl with huge boobs. I chugged Nyquil, gazed at ceiling tiles, conspired to give tit for tat, but really I just sat it out till fall, made my move after a football game. He came. *He came back.*

4. He used to stick my entire fist, all the way to the wrist,

in his mouth. I nicknamed him my monkey head. Followed him to frat parties, grad school, multiple Midwest moves. Lugged boxes of stuff from state to state. Told him we couldn't wait on perfect timing or other people's stance on *where we stood.*

5. We alternated shifts when the baby cried. Adjusted our expectations, sleep schedules, lives. We plowed through Iowa-ian winters, wind chills that made us curse, *fuck this fucking snow.* We were cold, but we survived seventy below, *figured out our unknown.*

6. And now we still, go on and on. Our children grow— we watch them waver their course. Our hearts brim over with knowledge, of course, of how love should be, and how it is not, and how a fine line can often be crossed. So, we interlace fingers, pray their luck will not end, that they'll find another soul that can bend with assiduous desire—to *weather the winters and weather the fire.*

THE ICE SWIMMER

A *whoop* pierced the quiet of her Glade Grove home. Sharon flicked long, white hair out of her eyes and stiffly kicked the covers aside, almost thankful for a reason to get out of bed. Her new meds had kept her awake well past an acceptable hour. She gripped her metal cane like a bat, peeked out the window. The half moon illuminated the gardenias along her fence.

Richard Morganson fell over the back gate, lay on the ground for a minute before strolling through her yard to stand unsteady by the pool. He pulled his shirt over his head, tossed it into the water. *What in the world?* A man their age acting like a teenager. He untied his lounge pants.

She snapped the blinds shut, thought about calling the police. It was so late. She cracked the blinds and leaned forward, pushing her nose against the pane. He was completely naked. She snapped the blinds closed. Held her breath. Opened the blinds again. He wavered on the edge of the pool, then hollered *whoop* and cannonballed into the deep end.

She rubbed her aching hip. It was three in the morning for Christ's sake. She couldn't call the police. What if they pulled up with sirens? Everybody on the street would come out, see them drag their naked neighbor out of her pool. Scandalous. The cops would probably pay as much attention to her as her pool company. She'd left four messages for them to come drain and cover the damn thing before the algae completely ate it up. No, thank you. Let the damn fool swim out there in his birthday suit, maybe he'd do her the favor of drowning. Then she'd really have to call the police. She'd deal with that at a decent hour. She steadied her cane by the bed, climbed in facing the window, and drifted to sleep. Only an occasional *whoop* jarring her slumber.

The next morning Sharon checked the backyard for any dead bodies before stepping out front to get the paper. Jay, a Hispanic model in his twenties who'd hit it big with a Calvin Klein underwear ad and moved into the stucco next door, was pruning the rose bushes that bordered their properties.

"Hey, lady. How're you this glorious morn?"

He waved the shears in a come-hither motion. She wished she'd had a second cup of coffee, as she picked up the newspaper and walked over.

"Sleepy."

"Stayed up late watching the show?" He raised his eyebrows and nodded toward the other side of his house, where Richard Morganson's Tudor home sprawled.

"You saw?"

"How could I not? All the whooping and nakedness, it was like a gay siren call."

"If it happens again, I'm calling the police."

"Why ruin the fun, child? It was *not* a hideous display, if you know what I mean."

She rolled her eyes.

"Shar Shar, *please*. I haven't had a date in months."

"I don't believe that for a second."

"Shh, shh. Here he comes." He fluttered his shears over the

roses like he could trim them using magic.

Richard walked to his Aston Martin, flipping his keys. His suit as slick as a commercial, but his hair rumpled. He looked like he could use another cup of coffee, too.

Jay raised his voice to carry over the lawns. "Hello, Dick."

Richard waved absentmindedly. "Hey, Jay…Shar." He flashed a mischievous smile before driving off.

"Damn, that man's too sexy to be so old."

Sharon swatted his arm with the paper.

"What? I can't help it. I've got daddy issues."

"That's disgusting."

Jay kissed the air. "You know you love me." He snipped a rose off the bush and handed it to her, which she placed in a finger vase on her kitchen windowsill. She poured herself that second cup of coffee, sat looking past the flower to the pool going green in her backyard.

Not again. She'd finally gotten to sleep before midnight. Now, only an hour later, she'd been awakened by whooping and splashing intermingling with her dreams. So she had left the window cracked—it was unseasonably warm for a September night in Richmond. She had every right to let in some air without being accosted by an unruly man. A man who didn't know the meaning of the word *decency.*

She'd show him. She grabbed her robe, tied the sash over her newest nightgown. The one she'd bought yesterday from that frilly store in the mall that she'd always been too embarrassed to shop in. She'd informed the saleslady that she wanted something tasteful, preferably with lace.

She stormed downstairs, her heart racing, opened the French doors and marched across the patio. Stood there, with hands on hips, while he swam. He didn't say a word, just kept swimming.

"What the hell do you think you're doing?"

He swam past her.

"It's the middle of the night."

He reached the far side, kicked off, and started the backstroke.

"You're a grown man. Completely naked."

He treaded water, staring at the aluminum ladder below her. He mumbled something.

"What?" she snapped.

"I love you."

He'd lost his mind. Did he have Alzheimer's? *"Are you drunk?"*

"Mama, let me stay."

"Don't call me mama. You need to get out of my pool or I'm calling the police."

He started the backstroke again, quietly whooping until he skidded over the entry steps, arms flailing. He sat up sputtering, a dazed look marring his handsome features.

Sharon clapped her hands. "Great performance. I give it an eight out of ten."

"What am I doing here?" He looked down and covered his privates with cupped hands.

"Are you serious?"

"What am I doing here?"

"How should I know? You took a dip in my pool last week and now tonight."

"Naked?"

"Stark."

He staggered out of the pool. "Could you at least get me a towel?"

"Follow me." She stomped into the house and down a hall. She came back with a forest-green towel, tossed it to him where he stood dripping on her tile.

"Thanks." He dried off briskly, then wrapped the towel around his hips, still shivering.

"I'll make some hot tea."

"I'm not exactly a tea man."

"Tonight you are." She turned on her Keurig. A few minutes later they each held a warm cup.

He wandered into the connecting den, perused the built-in beside the fireplace and her collection of trophies. He whistled low. "You've got a hell of a stash."

She flipped a switch by the mantle, the fire logs blazed.

"Is that an Olympic medal? This is yours?" At her nod, he gave another low whistle. "You mean to tell me, all this time I've lived two doors down from an Olympic gold medalist and didn't even know?"

"It was a long time ago."

"Still." He had a fine matting of chest hair. When he lifted his cup to his lips, his biceps bunched in a way that made Sharon's stomach clench.

"Did you know you sleepwalked?"

"I did as a kid, for a while after my dad died. I haven't since then."

"Until now."

"Until now." He nodded. "I've had someone come into my life. You know when you connect with someone you didn't expect to." He looked at her mouth.

She tightened her robe.

"Anyway, my dad passed when I was twelve. I'm sixty-seven now, ten years older than how I remember him." He picked up a trophy, hefted the weight, read the inscription out loud. "St. Petersburg Invitational."

"I got that for a triple Salchow. Back in 1968 it was impressive. Now it's expected in each routine, basic. Someone beat it four years later with another half rotation."

"Must suck, someone younger making your record obsolete."

"I suppose other people still have dreams."

He placed the trophy back on the shelf. "I don't care about other people's dreams." His gaze traveled from her eyes to her mouth. "I like your hair short," he said, but he was still looking at her lips.

Sharon smoothed her tousled chin-length new cut, leaned forward. She snatched his cup from the mantle behind him, walked to the kitchen.

He pointed to a photo of her on the ice. "You were a looker."

"Thanks," she answered deadpan, set the cup down with a clatter in the sink.

"No, I mean you're still attractive."

"It's okay, I know what you mean. I look good for my age."

"You never had children?"

"I had too many medals to win to make time for babies."

"I hear you. I had too many models."

She walked over, straightened a trophy with a slight twist. "Well, there's a difference."

"Is there?" He unloosed the towel from his hips, folded it with a cocky grace, and tossed it over the arm of her couch. "Thanks for the tea. It was good getting to know you, neighbor." Then he must have walked out the front door because all she heard was a click and when she opened her eyes, he was gone.

The next day broke sunny and crisp. A persistent knocking woke her. Richard stood at her door with a bouquet of roses that looked suspiciously familiar.

"You put words in my mouth last night. You do look good for your age. What I meant is you've got a refined grace you don't often find nowadays."

He pushed the flowers at her. "Thanks for dealing with me last night."

"Come in and have some coffee."

"I can't, I have to meet someone. I just wanted to clear that up. Go skating with me." He added, "Ice Zone downtown has public skate this weekend."

She clutched the flowers to her chest. "It'll be crowded."

"We'll weave in and out."

"I haven't put on a pair of skates in a dozen years."

"It's like riding a bike."

"I've got my cane."

"I'll hold your hand."

She buried her nose in the flowers. Their sweetness made her heart race.

"Okay." She beamed, her face matching the day.

"Good. I'll pick you up, noon on Saturday."

She lingered on her front step as Richard walked away with a nod to Jay, who was speed walking by him and up her walk.

"Ooooh, child, what'd he say? Love the sassy haircut, by the way. You look like a seventy-year-old pixie."

"Please." Sharon shook her head but couldn't suppress her smile. Jay went down and back up in a squat.

"You're a little minx. I want to be you when I grow up."

She swatted him with her bouquet. "He asked me out."

"Careful, you know his penchant for anorexic models young enough to be his daughter."

Her smile faded. He did another squat.

"I saw one just the other day, snooping around his place."

"When was that, during *your* snooping?"

"I see how it is, now that you're dating nineteen seventies' Golden Boy." Jay bent for another squat.

"What're you doing?"

"I've got my own hot date tonight, need to be tight. You're not the only sexy thang on the block."

She laughed. He blew her a kiss and sauntered back to his place.

A couple more times that week Richard went swimming. She didn't wake him, just listened from her bed with the window open. Once or twice she'd get up and tiptoe over, like he might hear her from the second floor, took a peek to ensure his safety. One time he woke up while swimming. He crested the water after a dive, looked up at her window with that grin. The other time he never woke up. She walked quickly outside on protesting hips and followed him when he left her yard. She'd feel awful if he died on her watch, the inconsiderate bastard. She ran hands over the gooseflesh skin of her arms as she scuffled in the moonlight across Jay's yard and back to her own front door after Richard had safely closed his.

On Saturday morning Sharon set her alarm for the first time since she could remember. She had already showered and dressed when the doorbell rang. An attractive blonde woman held a little girl's hand. Sharon guessed the girl was five or six, with hair the color of a penny. A slight smattering of freckles bridged her nose, adorableness on her front stoop.

"I'm sorry to bother you. I was hoping you'd give this to Richard?" The woman gestured toward his place. "He's not home and I don't want to leave it at his door." A thick photo album rested in the crook of her arm. "It's important."

"Okay."

The woman wiped at her eyes. "I'm sorry. I'm more emotional than usual, reconnecting with Richard and the pregnancy hormones." She rubbed her tightly rounded stomach.

"Oh."

"I just…do you mind? I thought he should have this…see Ava grow up, all the things he missed the first time around."

"Well, he'll see this one born." Sharon took the album, gripping it hard.

"You think so? I want him in their lives, but he can be a hard man to deal with."

"I understand."

After they left, Sharon changed into sweats and scrubbed her bathroom clean. When Richard showed up at noon, she handed him the album at the door.

"You met Heather? What'd you think?" Did he actually expect her to comment on his girlfriend.

"She's gorgeous, but the reason you need to be there is Ava." She shut the door and left him holding the album, his face blank.

As soon as the construction trucks arrived on Glade Grove his naked swims dried up. They'd meet occasionally on Jay's front lawn, make small talk. Nothing out of the ordinary, but she had the growing suspicion he was hiding something. She'd catch glimpses of his mischievous grin. Even though Heather's car was parked in his driveway more and more lately, he still flirted with Sharon. She didn't take it seriously. The incompetent pool company had finally come by and drained her pool, leaving it uncovered and a note on the bill that they'd be back to fix the pump and filter. She worried she'd find Richard lying at the bottom with his head cracked open.

Speculation on the street grew over Richard's construction project. Most guessed it was a cabana house for his young lover, a married runaway beguiled into leaving her husband by Richard's sinful ways and money. Anytime a neighbor braved the subject, he'd say, *you'll see,* with a smirk and leave it at that. Jay was bursting with curiosity and admitted spying over Richard's security fence, only to see temporary walls and tarps covering the entire backyard. One afternoon, Sharon tripped walking around a cement truck parked in front of her mailbox. Jay and Richard practically came to blows over who'd drive her to the hospital. In the end, she snapped at Richard to stop making a scene in front of Ava, and picked Jay. The hospital ordered an MRI, the radiologist shocked at the arthritis in her hips. A wheelchair was issued at checkout.

Jay rallied a group of neighbors to build a ramp for Sharon's front door with the help of his new boyfriend, a construction worker he'd met while peering over Richard's fence. Sharon mouthed *thank you* from the window, then closed the front curtains. She didn't have the heart to go out there. Among the workers she'd seen Richard and his girlfriend, smiling at each other while he handed her a hammer.

Sharon's chest felt tight. Her trophies winked at her from across the room. She rolled her wheelchair over to the largest one, staggered out of her chair to snatch it up and carry it shakily to the kitchen trash can. She held it over the lid, clenching the gold until her knuckles turned white. A blur in her peripheral vision caused her to glance out the window over the sink to the backyard. Ava bounced on the diving board.

"Ava!" Sharon screamed, slamming the trophy on the counter and bolting toward the patio doors. She flung the doors open, still yelling Ava's name. If anything happened to that child, she didn't know what she'd do. Ava swayed on the board. Sharon stumbled and fell to the patio. A second later, Richard ran through the side gate in what seemed like slow motion, and Sharon had the thought that they had all dived underwater. The child regained her balance and stood stiff on the board. Richard yanked her against his chest, panic dissipating as he walked back to Sharon. Heather, a few steps behind Richard, grabbed Ava from him and kissed her repeatedly on her freckles. Richard sat down beside Sharon, put his hand on her thigh.

Ava cried, hugged her mother. "Sorry, Mama."

"You scared Grandpa, too."

"Sorry, Grandpa." Ava smiled down at Richard, patted his head.

"Grandpa?" Sharon looked incredulously at Richard. His patent grin teased the corners of his mouth.

"Who did you think I was?"

One night, a few weeks later, he showed up at her door. "Come on. I've got something to show you."

He wheeled her down the street and up the walk to his backyard. When he opened his gate she gasped. An ice-skating rink shone under strands of twinkle lights strung from poles. It dazzled.

Ava and Heather smiled from the other side of the rink, holding hands and wobbling.

"I built it for you."

"How in the world?"

He whispered in her ear, "I'm loaded, baby." Sharon breathed in his scent—mint and spice.

"I don't understand. I can't skate. I can't even walk."

He pushed her wheelchair onto the ice, leaned down again to whisper, "I've been practicing my moves."

Richard spun and twirled her around under the lights that glistened like snowflakes, while Ava's laughter jingled in the night air. It might not have been worthy of an Olympic gold medal, but the sparkle in Sharon's eyes flashed brighter than all the trophies she'd ever won.

TECHNICALLY RELATED

I click off Flappy Birds, switch to Ancestry dot com.
Trace along the flight of my ancestors, a curved
green line—like the rolling hills from where we
came. Befriend my great-grandfather's descendants
in hi-def, peer into megapixels on Facebook profiles
for resemblance, wonder if I should ask about their
present or my past.

Most still live a country away, although today an
ocean closer. One lady I found the next town over,
a third or fourth half cousin. Her grandmother's
adoption, a mystery we investigate. No one ever
mentioned it, she explains. I give her the biological
last name that she had never heard spoken. Her
grandmother passed years ago, yet even she wouldn't
know—there's no one alive to ask.

I click and clack, peruse Find a Grave dot com.
Get confused. Plod along, until on my billionth
hyperlink I get a hunch, the farther I track back—
the more words go missing. I may never know why
my grandfather traded daughters, like he could copy
and paste lives. Genetically, if it saved me, perhaps

I shouldn't question. Even as time blurs, I'm learning
the truth of it—

a little bird delivered a tweet: the deeper my browser
history, the more every connection becomes relevant.

AIN'T NOTHING BUT A CHICKEN WING

Yes, I found Jesus while doing drugs. He turned up on a barstool beside mine in Hanalei. The facial hair gave him away. I'm not exactly legal, but the bartender thinks I'm pretty despite the burns, so he lets me sit at the bar. Jesus leans in and whispers, "Hey, I've got a secret for you." The smell of cannabis, goat cheese, and desperate religion knocks me off my stool, and I know my life is about to change.

He drives a VW wagon. Says he resurrected it from the auto graveyard near Wailua State Park. Says he can get me higher than God if I just stick around. On the drive to his place he preaches. Quotes lines from an old Edie Brickell song. Then asks if I know what he means. My phone buzzes and it's Mom telling me to come back home. Go by Frankie's first, she needs cold medicine. I promise her I'll be there when I can, cross my heart. Jesus doesn't mind stopping at the store. I go in. Tell Frankie it's been thirty days and he has to give me a goddamn box. Then I'm back in the wagon with Jesus. I tell him Mom needs her pills, but he just keeps driving.

The road ends beside a twenty-four hour hot wings drive-thru. We park in the lot behind it, beside a trailer and a couple of cars, all on blocks. The screen door hangs by one hinge and a few of the island's feral chickens are inside. Jesus shoos them out. A naked lady paints a man sprawled on a beanbag. He's only got one arm, a bucket of hot wings between his legs. Waves one at me in welcome, sauce dripping.

Crazy Keoni's toking off a pipe in the shape of a hula dancer, her pineapple headdress the bowl. He's sucking on her toes. Jesus nods me over to the Polynesian on the futon, and we pass the hula girl around. Everybody in town knows who Crazy Keoni is, but I've only ever seen him behind the coffee shop talking to chickens.

One thing you need to know about me, I don't smoke anything if it ain't organic. I don't want nothing you have to cook up. I've seen what that shit can do. I want my teeth. I want my soul. I know Mom's waiting, but this stuff in the hula pipe's as easy as Sunday morning. Smells like cotton sunshine hanging on the line. When she calls again I listen, see her speckled face like she's got a permanent case of chicken pox. She's begging me to come dig the bugs out from under her skin. I nod at the end. Disconnect.

Jesus is delivering a sermon about the white man invading the islands, taking all the decent land and converting it to resorts and gated communities. He gets up and pulls a red frame off the wall, hands it to me. I can see it's an airline ticket from Kauai to Wisconsin. His real name's Bernie Johnson. He came for holiday with his girlfriend's family and never left. Says he was just born in the wrong spot. Ignore the white skin, he's really Polynesian. He yanks the frame out of my hand and smashes it against the floor, says, "Nah, man, you have to feel this. Hold it in your hand."

Crazy Keoni's handing me the hula pipe at the same time, so I double fist it and the ticket. "You're holding freedom." Jesus stares at me for like an hour, but that might just be the pot. I pass both to him. Close my eyes. My phone's buzzing nonstop against my hip, and I know there's someplace I'm supposed to be. Another line from Brickell's "What I Am" drifts through my head and I see Mom cooking ice, heaving me on the step stool and telling me to stir—smells of cat piss and burnt plastic crawling down my throat, swallowing me.

At dawn, a rooster crows from the futon. I get off the floor. Naked lady and one-arm guy are gone. Jesus is snoring on the beanbag. Crazy Keoni's sharing the futon with the loud cock, until it jumps off, skitters over, and pecks Jesus on the beard, like it's digging for worms. He smiles for a second then bats him away, says he'll be putting sauce on him later if he doesn't watch out. I've got twenty-eight missed calls from Mom. She hasn't been sleeping, needs me to bring that cold medicine. Still, we pour Captain Crunch straight from the box into our mouths. Pack another bowl and pass it back and forth, critiquing the jokes on the cereal box. When we're convinced they've hired commie Japanese spies to brainwash an American generation, we slam out the screen door. It bangs against the trailer siding, crumpled beer cans jingling out with us.

We shuffle across the Kuhio Highway and we're at Kee Beach. Warning signs greet us with the dangers of rip currents, sudden drop-offs, high surf, and slippery rocks. Jesus keeps walking past the warnings, to the Kalalau trailhead. We climb for about an hour. Only pass three tourists, it's early yet. The trail's serious shit. A red clay path with jagged rocks sliced along the sheer cliffs of the mountain ridge, blanketed with rainforest palms. If I wasn't so high, the height would scare me.

I've scraped palms, dirty knees. I'm starting to think Jesus may not be the world's savior after all. But he keeps going higher, pushing me forward. We crest on a peak that juts out over the Pacific Ocean, does a sharp bend, then begins its descent toward

Hanakapiai Beach. I tell him to go ahead, I want to stay, and he just keeps walking. Doesn't even turn to say good-bye.

I lean out a little ways, awed by the rugged coastline. Green mountains etched with wild ridges, like the fingers of creation reached down and molded them. Thin slivers of silver course through from the nighttime rains. Orchids pop out from crevices nearby, and I marvel at how life clings to such a precarious perch. Plus, the sea is so damn blue. If I dive into it, it wouldn't be so bad.

I settle on the edge of my cliff, feet dangling. A chicken walks up from around the bend, sits down beside me. It's the whitest chicken I've ever seen, almost seems to glow. And when it turns to look at me, its eyes are blue. Its wings are too long for a chicken and I tell it so. I swear the thing smiles at me, a little condescendingly. Says, *Lana, do not be afraid. Aloha means good-bye, hello, and peace.* My phone buzzes and I dig it out of my pocket. Offer it to her like chicken feed. Her beak is sharp. When she pecks my hand, my palm bleeds, making my burns look faded. She flies off over the sea and the buzzing disappears.

I squint, searching across the waves. Marvel. Wonder over freedom in a frame and prophets on barstools. Look down over the path I've circled up. Think about all the places I could go. Think about Wisconsin. Anticipate the scent of snow.

SUNDAES AND APPLE PIE

Did you hear, McDonald got arrested? SWAT
team swarmed during dinner rush, clogged
the drive-thru line. Said, *Hey, Mac, you're
coming with us.* A scuffle ensued…golden
fries strewn, soda flung like tear gas when he
resisted. He might have got away, if he hadn't
slipped in a grease spot, so officers blocked
an employee entrance. It's not like he'll fry,
charged with reckless endangerment. Head-
lines blared: *Hardened criminal arrested,
prosecution seeks thirty to life.* Bet he'll counter,
pay the price of a Big Apple lawyer. The mug
shot's online, painted-on-smile smudged. It's not
every day, though, you see a clown thrown in
the slammer, wig knocked askew. Super-sized
shoes drug two arteries thru the disarray like
notebook lines all the way to the squad car, kids
scrambling behind, snatching *made in China* toys—
happily, like writing *land of the free* as evidence
of the clown's constitutional rights.

While they're at it, hope they investigate that chicken
joint, swear they put crack in those sandwiches.

DAILY RATION

We are fortunate. Abundance surrounds us. We are buried in resource, an unlimited supply.

I zip up my orange chore boots. Double-check that the Time-2Monitor on the kitchen wall is flashing *Field Duty*. Sync my matching wristband. Tap the screen. It's been on the fritz since the reaping party, when we celebrated the end of the picking-up period, all those months of separating items blown into the fields from the dumping grounds. In the middle of Dad's thankful speech my monitor went blank, long enough for my heartbeats to rise above acceptable level. An automatic report would have been generated and sent to Central Data, whose Time2 experts take care of us. I don't need to worry.

My boots clomp on the farmhouse floorboards weakened with age. I snatch my day goggles off the nail by the front door, pat my jacket pocket to check I have my air mask, and step outside. Central Data has not restructured our home, yet. Off-white paint flecks from the clapboard siding. I run my hand along the porch rail, the roughness reminds me of cat tongues. A couple of flakes stick to my palm. I bend over, take shallow breaths, straighten and search the gray horizon.

Dad and Remee are already in the fields. Two specks moving among the towering off-white bales. Dad stands out blue against the slick rolls of harvest. Remee is climbing halfway up one. He's eleven, five years younger than me. *Almost six*, I think. My birthday will be celebrated in two weeks. My Easy Cake delivered, the top lit, and the oxygenator used to blow it out. All heated to a goopy bowl of sweetness. My stomach rolls over. I try not to think about what I found under the loose floorboard in my bedroom.

Dad points in my direction and Remee jumps off his perch, waves and hollers, *Wendee*. Runs toward me across the large dry field. We won't have any problem keeping the fires lit today. The rapeseed oil truck is pulled up to the metal burn barrels. My brother stops midway and bends over, trying to settle his breathing. No doubt reminded by the flashing from his wristband. I can see his shoulders shake with cough. My chest tightens. He soon recovers, walks fast toward me, skinny arms pumping. When we meet, his straw-colored hair sticks out in wild disarray and I can't resist giving it a ruffle. He looks like the scarecrow in the history lesson, *The Wizard of Oz*. I'm reminded to be grateful for what I have.

Remee's excited about the melting. We'll each get extra rations. Dad moves slower among the rolled bundles. We celebrated his thirty-seventh birthday six months ago. We are thankful. He has surpassed expected lifespan. I walk faster to make up the remaining distance, wrap my arms around his barrel chest. The top of my head brushes his chin and I inhale deeply. His sweat smells metallic, but I catch a faint whiff of earth and skin, like faded memory.

He says, *Come, Sunshine. Let's get to work.* I don't understand his nickname for me, but it makes me smile just the same. We head over to the nearest bale to the farm road. As we get closer the pale heap morphs into specifics: plastic straws, forks, cups, lids, and, of course, the plastic bags that tie it all together in tight layers. Drinking straws stick out helter-skelter and snag at my midnight hair. I brush them aside. It's the forks you have to watch out for; they'll scratch you, especially the ones with broken tines. Dad checks each roll for hidden syringes, but they're heavier and don't usually blow out this far. The farms closer to the city have to be more vigilant. I'm good at finding things. The trick is to let yourself blur until all distractions bleed away and you're left seeing what's really in front of you. Dad says it's a gift, but I'm not so sure.

An image of rusty nails and uneven floorboards pried up looms over the field. I shake my head, clear my thoughts of buried boys with rumpled hair and reaching hands. There's work to be done. Remee races ahead again, to the burn racks. Dad and I laugh as we put our backs into heaving the first bale over. The oil truck driver is watching a show on his wristband, an old Vinny and Verve episode. The one where Vinny gets mad at Verve for ruining his favorite pair of shoes, a worn-out pieced-together pair from his grandfather. Verve makes up for it by molding him a better pair, indestructible and shiny new. It's a pretty good episode, but I still think it's rude the driver doesn't say *hi* when we walk over. Maybe Central Data should add *Manners* to the interface.

A second truck is coming up the farm road, trailing dust like factory smoke. The oil truck driver's show cuts off, replaced with orange directions. It is time. He flips a chrome switch on the back of his truck and rapeseed oil oozes through a tube into the barrel. We shove the bale over the lip of the burn rack and clang the door shut, while the second truck backs up and locks into the sloped tubing coming from the barrel. This driver is friendlier. He grins and takes his air mask off to show us. Says,

What a beautiful day, and throws his free hand out to indicate the desiccated fields. Then covers his mouth with the mask once more, gets back in the truck to wait. In red bubble lettering on the side of the black truck, it says, DAILY RATIONS SERVED TO YOU! There's a picture of a man in a flat cap, smiling and pointing presumably at the *you* in the slogan. He's wearing some kind of white uniform with a red collar my dad once whispered was a *bow tie*. It's kind of creepy, in a funny way, and I clutch Remee to me. Tell him to back away from the heat.

My dad pours ChemoMix into a tube that empties into the burn barrel. It starts the melting. Then he throws a packet of kerosene over the lip of the barrel, and flames shoot out like tongues. Remee says, *Wow*. I take his air mask from his jacket pocket and secure it properly over his nose and mouth, snap it closed behind his head. Then I do the same with mine. I pull Remee closer, so his back rests against my stomach, and my arms cross over his chest. The bale burns quick and fierce like the lightning storms that roll out from the city and crash the fields each night. Frightening and beautiful at the same time. A cloud of black smoke mushrooms above the barrel, intact like a living creature, and then merges with the lighter gray sky. The fine hairs on my arms tingle under my jacket, but I don't let go of Remee to rub them.

Dad still hasn't put on his mask. He's wearing it less and less since his birthday. He leans over to me and tells me to take mine off—*It'll make you stronger*. I reach up with one hand, yank it from my mouth, letting it hang around my neck. He's right. I haven't gagged during harvest for several years now. Not like when I was younger. When my parents worried that I wasn't an adaptor. During trial age, when I would either grow or wither away like rotten floorboards in nonrestructured houses.

There's a spout near the sloped tubing that the daily rations truck is attached to. Dad pulls out our metal cups, stacked one in the other, from his work jacket's pocket. Soon, Dad and I will push another bale over to burn. But with the first bale of the harvest we have a family tradition. He hands Remee and me our cups. The metal feels slick and I'm again reminded of the thing I found. How the glossy paper felt sturdy and fragile at the same time. My cheeks burn, remembering the slickness as I rubbed the image, traced faces with my fingertip. Squinted at plates and bowls laid on a farmhouse table. The same table we use to store our work boots when not on field duty. There are odd things heaped on the plates. I think they are different foods, but I can't recognize any of them and there are no delivery boxes. About half a dozen people smile, staring straight out of the paper. A couple look comically ancient, like the ragtag pair of Vinny's shoes. A boy, about Remee's age, has his head slightly turned. He's reaching toward a blue bowl stacked with round things the color that lightning storms leave on closed eyelids. On his face sits an expression I can't quite name. I'm sure he's supposed to wait. I can't stop wondering.

The back of the glossy paper is rougher, and someone has written directions in a strange flowing font. They don't make any sense. I wonder if it's a foreign tongue, but I recognize this house and some of the words, like *grandma's*, *cup*, and *stir*. I shake my head. I should be concentrating on our harvest tradition. But the image and swirling words are burned into my mind like the black creature the barrel birthed is now part of the stone sky.

Dad opens the spout and Remee and I hand him our cups to fill. He pours them to the top with the off-white liquid, hands them back to us one by one. He pulls out our InstaDrink tablets to sink in the hot sludge so that our insides won't be damaged. Usually we have to wait for the cooling process to complete, add more ChemoMix to thin it out. Today, on the first bale of the harvest, we get to drink our ration fresh from the spout. Remee holds his cup high, eager for Dad to add the InstaDrink. His expression is a mirror of the boy that I found. My throat closes. I swallow, choke on my talent of finding.

PRETTY ENOUGH

His fork scrapes against a dinner plate in his lap, while an anchorwoman's mouth moves in mute circles on the fat, out-of-date TV. The maroon fabric of his recliner has faded to a musty shade of pink, but she knows better than to tell him.

"Hey, Dad." She gives a small wave from the doorway, soccer ball under an arm and hair in a messy ponytail.

"You're home late."

"Coach wanted me to talk to a scout after the game, maybe get a scholarship." She sits on the couch, rubbing her hip. The glare of the TV flashes over his worn face, brightening it like makeup.

"Scholarship?" He shovels another forkful into his mouth, talks around it. "Girls' soccer's not a real sport."

She yanks off dirty cleats, tugs down shin guards to hang like tongues poking out her socks.

He grunts. "They probably cry if they break a nail on a throw-in. Manchester United. Now that's real soccer."

She scrutinizes her bloody knee. Jabs around the jagged edge. "Maybe you could come watch a game. There's plenty of space in the bleachers."

He clicks the remote. The anchorwoman drones about a local teenager raped. "You should be a cheerleader. You're pretty enough," he says, still looking at the screen.

She limps to the kitchen for an ice pack. Stands in front of
the refrigerator. Studies her stainless-steel reflection.

WISH YOU WERE HERE

She only had an hour to make her connecting flight, but Le Marteau was his favorite restaurant and he wanted to talk. He stood when he saw her. Stiff bristles around his mouth pricked her cheek when she leaned in for a kiss. His navy suit smelled like starch, mirrored her own. A platter of escargot grew cold on the table.

"I ordered for us."

She clamped a shell with steel pinchers, dug at the meat with a cocktail fork.

He pulled a hammer from his lap and laid it between them. "How's Greg?"

"Why do you have a hammer, Dad?" The metal head glinted, winking at her.

"It was your grandfather's. I don't want it thrown out when I'm gone. Greg should have it."

Garlic butter from the snails glistened on his lips. She tried to remember her grandfather pounding nails into planks but could only picture her grandmother slicing ham. "I doubt they'll let me carry it on the plane."

"Well, your brother's already got a garage full."

Ice clinked in her glass, reminding her of tea glasses sweating in both hands. Watching her younger brother fix a mower, their dad explaining to him how to exchange broken blades for whole ones.

Her father wiped the cloth napkin across his mouth. "How's the job search?"

"Slow. He's been talking about consulting work."

"It can be hard on a man."

"I know it's hard. It took me half a year when we moved to Tulsa for Greg's grad school."

"Sure, but it's different for a man."

She chewed an escargot. They had overcooked it. She touched the wooden handle of the hammer, smoothed from years of her grandfather's hand clutching it, swinging and smashing things. *It's different for a man*, the exact words the girls had used at happy hour last week, after she confessed to looking at Greg's phone— finding texts. *Boys will be boys. Survival of the species.* Platitudes to make her feel better about staying. Again.

The waiter cleared the appetizer dishes. He came back with the entrees her father had ordered, called him by name.

Her father cut into his rib eye. "Greg should fly down to the lake house. We could fish, grill out."

"God, I haven't been there since I was a kid."

"It'd be good for us to spend some time together while he's got the chance, male bonding."

She stabbed her salad. "I'll ask Greg."

He wiped at a spot on his suit sleeve, white lint from the napkin speckled the fabric. "How are you doing?"

"Great. I'm heading up a client presentation today in Dallas, hoping for a promotion."

"How do you think Greg's going to feel if you get promoted now?"

She speared a cherry tomato with her fork. "I don't know, Dad. Happy we have a paycheck?"

"I can lend you money if things are tight."

She bit into the tomato. Its juices bled across her tongue. She gripped the hammer handle and hefted its weight, wondered how it felt to slam it.

"I'd better go."

"You haven't eaten."

"I have to make my flight. You could have just called Greg."

"I want you to deliver the hammer."

"You could have mailed it!" She flung it to the table. The claw nicked her plate and a chip flew.

"Don't cause a scene, honey."

She stood and pushed her chair in. Snatched the hammer, again. "Don't get up. Finish your steak."

They stopped her at security, searched her body. Men asked her about the hammer. She tried to explain it like her dad would, but she didn't know how. A security officer called his boss, Mr. Matthews, who came fifteen minutes later on a beeping cart. He had to approve it. There was a form to appeal for permission to carry it instead of tossing the hammer in the garbage bins full of lotions, perfume bottles, and other discarded things. She missed her flight.

By the time she got to Dallas they were at cocktails. Her boss, Randy, told her how impressed he had been when Michael took charge of her presentation. In fact, even though she had trained Michael, he was promoting him to Senior Account Executive. He just had that persuasive confidence that connected with clients. She smiled and nodded, congratulated Michael, and thought about the hammer waiting in her carry-on.

At home that night Greg was asleep. She looked at his quiet mouth longingly and swung the hammer—hard, like her father taught her. When the policeman came she followed his orders. At the jail they searched her body. When the judge asked her why she had done it, she answered him, *Because it's different for a man.*

YOUR VOICE

It's good to hear your voice. I guess it's silly to keep calling this number. For a split second, I think you might actually pick up. There's so much I want to tell you.

Sophie's growing up so fast. Sometimes I feel like she's taking care of me instead of the other way around. Remember how I always had to bug her to brush her hair? Now she's reminding me to brush mine. She got a C in math. She has your math skills though, so I can't blame her. She cried when she handed me her report card. Like I could be upset over a grade after everything that's happened.

Eli doesn't care about school anymore. According to Peggy, that's a defense mechanism. I told you about her, our *family adjustment counselor*. Eli supposedly has "complicated grief." When she told me that, I laughed right there in her cheery little office. Complicated grief. Like grief could be simple. I kept laughing while she looked at me, waiting for me to either fall apart or get myself together. I was going to tell her about finding your old T-shirts balled up under the covers at the foot of Eli's bed, but I was so angry I kept my mouth shut. Eli acts like nothing bothers him, but most mornings those hazel eyes are red-rimmed. When I look in those eyes, I see you instead of him.

You would be proud of me. The insurance papers are filed and I've found a part-time job to help with the bills. The big things are covered. It's the little things that sneak up and knock me down, your side of the bathroom counter clean, nobody to laugh with at late-night TV.

If I tell you something, you have to promise not to be angry. I pressed a razor to my wrist and wondered if I could do it. Is it strange that those thoughts felt good? For about five seconds I didn't think of you at all. I'm sorry.

That's why this is my last phone call. I have to stop clinging to your absence, so I can hold on to the part of you that's still here. When I hang up I'm going to call the cell company and cancel this line. I know you'd understand.

I'm going to miss hearing your voice.

MAKING SPACE

Brian sips his coffee and surveys the room from the cool recesses of the doorway. Renovations have been achingly slow, but the completion snuck up on him just the same and the room is now changed. Maggie stands in front of a new bank of windows. An art easel, dragged out of a cramped corner of the attic, has been dusted off and dominates the space. Rose-colored light from the windows dapples his wife in pinks and grays, and he has the unexpected thought of the flowers on their wedding cake.

Everything here is slick with newness, white walls, honey-boarded floors, stainless-steel countertops loaded with paints in tubes stacked on racks and a sink for cleaning colors off brushes. Maggie wanted openness and light. Everything is different. Except for two chairs, if you can call them that, left over from an era when the space functioned as a playroom. Two sets of overstuffed padded vinyl blocks, one block standing on end behind the other flat on the floor, make lumbering resemblances of chairs. One set bright aqua, the other a god-awful orange. They sit slightly askew, looming like drunken dinosaurs in the corner trying not to be noticed. How long have they had those chairs, twenty years now? Maggie says she doesn't mind the mismatched relics, but she didn't give him too much grief when he put them on Craigslist.

He watches his wife add color to the canvas. The sharp swiping of the brush sounds surprisingly dry, faintly like backpacks zipping closed. The tang of the oil paints competes with his coffee.

"Let's go to Vegas." He breaks the silence, moves into the room a little.

"Vegas, where did that come from?" She glances at him over her shoulder.

"Why not? They won't miss me at work for a couple days. We could be on a plane by midnight."

"You're crazy." She laughs and turns back to her painting. It's her childhood home. A photo her mother took years ago pinned to the top of the easel for reference. He wonders if she misses the sting of the Day Dreamer Roses that lined the walk, or the sweet tang of lemonade on the front stoop, sticky afternoons piercing holes in metal tops of jars in anticipation of firefly-chasing evenings. Bits of fairytale childhood she used to describe to Max and Janie, back when they still asked for stories. The painting isn't very good; details are absent. She hasn't picked up a brush since the kids started elementary school, more than a decade ago.

Brian starts again. "Come on. It'd be fun. We could gamble a little. Catch a show. Stuff ourselves sick at the all-night buffets. Stay at the Bellagio, go all out."

"Brian, I've finally got the studio together. And what if Max or Janie needed us?"

He walks over to the sink, turns the water on and off, testing the new faucet. "Max's too busy partying with the Sigma Chis to even call, and Janie's obsessed with researching grad schools. I doubt they'll even know we're gone."

She dabs at the canvas, lightening the shade of bricks. She adds a touch of yellow, blends it until it's absorbed, and says, "Well, I'm not going to Vegas."

Brian rips off a paper towel from the holder beside the sink and wipes the spray left on the nozzle, the sink basin. It comes away a muddied red, already stained from her brush rinses. He walks down the hall, down the stairs to the kitchen and throws the wadded-up paper towel in the bin under the old sink there, pours more coffee into his mug. It's grown lukewarm from sitting. He zaps it in the microwave for a few seconds, picks up the paper from the counter. Puts it back down. He doesn't need the news. The grass could use mowing. Maybe he'll start paying that Herman kid to take care of it for him. His back hurts.

He checks the calendar hung on a nail over the recycle bin. A lady from Craigslist is coming to pick up the chairs between three and five. He has her number scrawled in the tiny white block for today. Why anyone would pay money for those chairs he hasn't the foggiest. It just proves you could put anything on there and someone would take it off your hands. She had sounded nice though, if a little frazzled with all the kids screaming, dog barking, and TV blaring on her end. He guessed he remembered those days of hectic activity and how much noise went along with it all. Personally, he'd bid good riddance to those loud, worn-out chairs.

Orange and aqua. Colors that used to be fashionable, now considered tacky. He could blame the kids. Max had insisted on aqua for no other reason than it was a boy color, and Janie had refused on the same grounds. She was daddy's girl, obstinate like him. Her hot head picked the orange. The chairs were basically four overeager building blocks. Max and Janie had transformed them into all sorts of things: rocket ships; theater stages; stepping stones above hot lava; fortresses—against aliens, zombies, policemen; circus rings; trampolines; 7-Eleven counters; airplanes; castles; and prison chambers. And those are just the days he can remember. Maggie probably remembers more.

Maggie says she's staying busy with her painting classes, chores. She says she's always wanted her own art studio. She certainly has been spending enough time up there lately. Says she's comfortable there. When he moves those chairs out, it'll give them more space. Maybe buy a plush recliner for him to read the paper, watch her work. Perhaps start that novel he's been meaning to write for years. A chair he could sit in for a while, not like those two. How Janie had fallen asleep every afternoon on them he had no idea, sleeping like the dead. He'd tickle her ribs until she chortled herself awake, his annoyance at supper growing cold washed away by finding her lying there so quiet. Those chairs were not made for grown men. They didn't give at all.

The material was cheap but it wiped off easy, which was a selling point. Now, the chairs were stained. Of course, they couldn't have foreseen Max's splatter phase, when he actually believed he could become Jackson Pollock if only he threw enough paint around. Once, Brian had tried to destroy the red, yellow, and black specks of creative liberty before Maggie got home. He must have said *shit* as he scrubbed. He didn't really remember that part, just looking up and Janie shaking her head, saying, *No, Daddy, you can only say this*, and making a pistol of her thumb and forefinger—shooting him. Maggie had chosen that moment to walk in. He should have known she would laugh off the Jackson Pollock fiasco; after all, Max was just like her.

Brian gets a second mug and pours coffee, heats it. He adds two spoonfuls of sugar, watching them dissolve in the black. He grabs the phone, carries it to the calendar, dials the Craigslist lady's number, and waits for her to pick up. Tells her he is *sorry, but the chairs are already sold.* It's all right. It is not really a lie. He's sure the woman on the other end of the line will accumulate her own mismatched chairs. In fact, he'd bet money she already owns them.

He climbs the stairs to the new studio, holds out the cup for Maggie. She can't resist strong sweet coffee. He nods to their chairs, says, *Come sit with me a minute.* He knows she will follow him, as he tries to ease onto the bright cushion. The vinyl gives a squeaky protest but is sturdy under his weight. He says, *How about we visit Alaska, instead? It's supposed to be clean and bursting at the seams with daylight.* He rubs her cheek, captures a sprig of curl resting there and gives a playful tug. He says, *We'll watch the glaciers calf blue ice into the waters. Maybe next spring would be nice.*

She answers, *Yes, now you're talking.*

SOMETHING FOUND

I wake up hard. It's the third time since my eightieth birthday, when I had closed my eyes and yellow candle pinpricks morphed into dead cows lying in snow. I don't know if it's a medical miracle or a last surge of adrenaline before an old man dies. It's achingly familiar, but the memories that tagged along I thought long buried.

It was the winter the cattle died. Winds reached speeds that beat my rusty Ford down the road. Women were afraid to walk from the kitchen to the chicken coop for fear of being blown through the badlands all the way down Highway 16 to Sioux Falls.

While Mrs. Wilson calculated algebraic fractions, I'd stared at the back of Virginia Fletcher's head all fall and into that biting winter. Her mama had brought her home from the hospital wrapped in pink just three days after my mama brought me home wrapped in blue, yet it had taken me sixteen years to notice the red hidden in her black hair.

The first catastrophic storm of that winter of '49 trapped Virginia and me in my rundown truck, together. We tried hunkering down, waiting it out. As the inches piled up in the bed and the gas needle's stamina dwindled, we knew we'd have to brave a path through the drifts.

A storm for the record books of Pennington County. I wasn't a man yet, but I tried to act like one. I busted into a ranch outpost with an axe to the door. It gave way easy after a couple thrusts, only evidence a few splinters fragmented and hanging from the catch. I pushed my way in and Virginia followed.

The next morning, when the snow finally stopped falling, I left her sleeping to walk outside on clean sheets. There was no blood, yet the cattle were lying on their sides, brown eyes staring back at me as if they had already forgotten.

Virginia and I swore we'd never forget that night, grateful for a burgeoning heat to stoke our shivers. I struggle to recall the exact combination of red and black in her hair, like it's a formula I can repeat. I'm not sure if the blankness that follows is from a neglected promise, or if I am just blinded by the brilliance of memory. I stare at my white in the toilet, and flush.

HELLUVAGUY

"How come everybody always says good things about dead guys?"

The barkeep, Johnny, sits on a stool beside his old high school buddy, toying with the edge of a soggy black napkin.

"JB Hollister was a bastard. I mean a real sonuvabitch. Everybody knows it. But he drops dead of a heart attack and, *boom*, all of a sudden he's a helluvaguy?" Bobby lifts his pint of beer in salute to either his dead friend or the apparent illogic of the world—it's unclear.

Johnny's bar is closed. They aren't supposed to serve alcohol on Sunday, not till after one o'clock, anyways. Johnny raises his glass halfheartedly and takes a sip. It tastes better than he remembered. He hasn't had a drink in seven years. He's probably served half a million drinks in that time and not had one drop. An accomplishment, really. Then Bobby called to say he was coming home to give JB's eulogy.

When Johnny called his grown daughter—she'd moved to Wisconsin over a decade ago—and told her JB had died, she said it was to be expected at their age. He guesses she's right. Seems like every weekend he picks up the paper and scans the obituaries for familiar faces, girls he dated growing up, friends he'd gone to school with who had moved away. It's like a game, the geriatric equivalent to I Spy. I spy Jim Flatford dead at seventy-two on page twelve. I spy Nancy Greene dead at sixty-eight on page thirteen. *God, it's hell getting old.*

Look at Bobby, sitting there in a shirt at least a size too small and four decades out of fashion, stretched across his thickened chest like it's trying to hold him together. The reds of the plaid washed and hung out to dry so many times they're now pink, softened with time, unlike them. Hell, he couldn't even find words to comfort an old friend, just show his support by lifting a pint.

Johnny picks up his beer and takes a bigger swallow, slams it back a little harder than he expected. "Sonuvabitch."

Bobby takes a swallow of his own beer, slams it down.

"Remember that time we all went down to Paddy's Creek to go skinny-dipping with Maggie Winfry and Amanda Robbins?" Bobby laughs. Johnny grins over his glass.

"We were what? Fifteen?"

"Yeah, and JB stole his daddy's work truck to pick up the girls."

Johnny is laughing now, too. "I'll never forget those girls' faces when he pulled up in that cement truck while they're trying to sneak out and hollered, *Come on, girls, we're ready to rooolllll.*"

"Sonuvabitch."

"Sonuvabitch."

Both men stare into their glasses.

"What time is it?"

Johnny turns his wrist, checks his watch. "Ten after."

"We're supposed to be there."

Johnny grunts agreement.

"We're supposed to greet people."

Johnny takes another gulp. So does Bobby.

Johnny turns to Bobby and smacks the back of his hand against

Bobby's plaid arm. "Hey, how long you have that shirt anyway? It looks older than you."

"I'll have you know this is the very shirt I wore when I picked Debbie up on our first date in 1964. Thank you very much."

Johnny whistles low. "Wow, vintage. I can't believe you still have it. Rebecca would have made me get rid of it a long time ago."

"Hell no, this is a classic. You can't even find these things nowadays. They don't make the fabric. Bleeding madras is history."

"Well, I think it's seen better days, buddy."

"Yeah, well, haven't we all?"

Johnny swigs another mouthful. So does Bobby.

"What you gonna say about JB?"

"I don't know. I guess about how big a sonuvabitch he was."

Johnny drains his beer. So does Bobby. They both look at the bottom of their glasses. Both want another. Both shake their heads and stand. Johnny says to leave the glasses, he'll come back later and clean up. He pats his friend on the shoulder as they head out the door. Bobby pats his friend back as Johnny locks up.

"Dammit, JB was a helluvaguy."

"Helluvaguy."

LESSONS IN REMEMBERING

She says, *We joined a new church and look what I found*,
lips flapping like a red flag declaring you her discovery.
You remember how she is.
From the directory, you smile at me again, glossed over
with time and tied up in a suit. I wouldn't have even
known it was you, if she hadn't of told me, standing in
the ladies' room of the theater, searching for a dry spot
to lay you in, then finally just holding you up to the light,
struggling to reconcile memories with colored pages.

She stands beside you, hand draped on your shoulder.

We promised we would never forget, down a dirt road
with only trees greened with restless anticipation to disturb
our lessons in remembering. When you taught me how to
bend and I taught you how to miss someone while they
were still standing in front of you.
Does the brush of her thigh when the preacher instructs
you to sit, remind you of forgotten touches in the back
of your car *(What color was it again?),* the one with the
cassette player that kept repeating?
Remember that time I said we should run off and get
married, and I knew you loved me because you said you

were just a country boy and you wanted more for me than
that? That I wouldn't be happy sitting in a worn farmhouse
with neighbors who owned chicken coops and rifle racks
in the back of pickup trucks.

You knew me then. These are some things I remember,
but they are dry like spent coals that break apart when
handled. *(Do ashes remember the flame?)*

I knew you then. I'm not sure if you remember, but I still
wonder when I look at her smile, what if that had been—me?

HEART'S ARTILLERY

Jasper's tail thumped against Henry's leg as they turned onto Thornberry Street. Henry hoped that crazy Jap lady wasn't out front scraping the pavement again. *Asian*, he thought. Becky would scold him, her light eyes scrunched in the same frown she'd had since she was a kid, forty-some-odd years ago. Hell, once he'd hit seventy, seemed like everybody had an opinion about how he needed to behave.

The houses on Thornberry held their posture firm like they were stiffened with age. The yards meticulously tamed and cut back except for the trees, which had outgrown their owners. Trucks blocked a neighborhood road at least once a week, hacking up an oak or a maple to make room for more sun and lawn. An older lady, in a heavy shawl, patrolled her flowerbeds, bending occasionally to pluck a weed. Henry waved to her and she gave a hesitant nod back. The neighborhood had been friendlier when Becky was small, running around with the other kids. Now the streets lay quiet.

Jasper whined. His butterscotch shoulders strained forward, sent a tug up the strap Henry carried to support the dog's hind legs.

"What is it, boy? You can't outrun those squirrels anymore."

The golden lab's nails raked against pavement in a frenzy of excitement rare for him these days. *Damn.* The Asian lady was in the street. He knew it was her, even squatted back on her heels wearing an oversized black jacket so faded it was gray, with a burgundy knit cap covering her still black hair.

All summer she'd kept a sharp eye on them when they walked past her yard. In September, she'd scolded Jasper for chewing a piece of trash in her ditch. She'd run across her lawn and jerked it from the dog's mouth. The next day, a magazine article had been taped to Henry's front door. Some fancy LA apartment building was using DNA testing to fine tenants who didn't pick up their dog's feces. He'd tossed it in the trash, avoided her block for a couple weeks.

Now, she was hunched over some stain, scrutinizing it. Jasper headed toward her, nose to the ground, tail waving furiously.

"No, no, dog!" The lady pushed at Jasper with her elbow out, blocking her face, and guarded the pavement with the spade she'd been using to scrape.

"Jasper. Calm down, boy."

The lab nudged his way under the lady's arm and licked her cheek. Henry thought he might have imagined the tight smile that appeared on her face, it vanished so quickly, as she exclaimed, "What's wrong with your dog?"

Henry yanked the dog back and stood a few feet away while she frantically scraped what turned out to be red chewing gum off the pavement. It stretched from the asphalt in sticky ribbons until they snapped, like tendons pulled taut. She scooped it in a plastic bag and ran her fingers along the top to seal it before standing to acknowledge them, like it was a damn baby or a hundred dollar bill.

"Nothing. He's just being curious."

She wrinkled her nose like Jasper needed a bath. There were fine lines around her mouth. He guessed she was close to his age.

She jabbed the air with her spade. "I don't want that dog's saliva on everything."

"It's just litter, lady."

She crossed her arms, glared at Henry like she was a five-foot samurai warrior.

"What are you doing with the gum?" Henry nodded to the bag she clasped.

She glanced at the bag then at Henry. "What's wrong with your dog? I see you walk him every day." She pointed to the harness on Jasper's back, the nylon strap that even now Henry held tight.

"Nothing." They were only a street over from home, but the lab sat at the word *nothing* and plopped down, head on paws like he needed a break. The lady regarded Jasper, her eyes squinched like she knew something or was trying to figure something out. Henry blurted, "Say, where are you from anyway?"

"Milwaukee."

Henry's laugh started in his gut and grew until his shoulders shook. He let go of Jasper's brace to hold his chest. Becky would lecture him for hours if she saw him laugh in this lady's face. Apparently, he was good at offending people when he didn't mean to. He studied his neighbor. Instead of the glare he expected, she was battling a grin. A giggle gushed out of her like bubbles in champagne rising, and Henry had the unexpected memory of flutes clinking before a kiss.

"That's even worse," Henry spit out and erupted with laughter again. He swatted his leg. "I'm sorry. My daughter would kill me."

At the word *daughter* the lady's laughter abruptly stopped, like a spigot twisted off. "I have to go. Get this processed." She gave a slight jerk of the hand that grasped the chewed gum and scurried up her driveway.

Jasper whined and stood up slowly. They headed home, Henry still carrying his comment, his laughter gone.

The next morning, mist hugged lawns like lovers reluctant to abandon their bed. Jasper stumbled to the door when Henry reached for his walking shoes. "There's no reason to be embarrassed," Henry muttered to himself as he tied shoestrings. "That crazy lady's scraping gum off pavement to be *processed*." Whatever the hell that meant. She was probably a nut. Most people from Milwaukee were.

He wasn't going to change his route anymore because of some old lady. Still, his gut tightened as he rounded the corner of Thornberry Street and scanned her yard and driveway. No one was out. It made sense with the weather. They cut their walk short, got out of the wet. Henry sat with the newspaper and another coffee, Jasper's nose resting on his knee.

Morning stretched into afternoon and Henry piddled with some bill writing and drawer organizing, until Jasper's whine at the door gave him a good excuse to let the clutter rest. They had a rule of only one walk a day—he didn't want to wear the old boy out, but the sun had banished the fog and the breeze carried a hint of jasmine that Henry knew must be his imagination this time of year. Still, it carried him off his porch and over a street to Thornberry where the lady paced, scouring the edges of her lawn for cigarette butts, gum, or discarded beer cans the teenagers threw out car windows before pulling in their own parents' driveways.

She looked up as they approached and this time smiled freely. Henry's pace quickened and Jasper gave a friendly bark, then stumbled, causing Henry to stutter-step and almost fall on the dog. He'd been carrying more and more of Jasper's weight, so that his arm ached after their walks. The smell of muscle cream permeated his sheets, kept him awake at night.

The lady reached out both arms like she could catch them. Henry regained his balance and stopped to let the lab rest.

"Is he okay?" She tilted her head, peered at Henry.

He considered her eyes, a rich mocha. The outer edges creased downward. The singsong voice of Becky, about age eight, floated through his head, *Chinese...Japanese...dirty knees,* and his face grew red. "No. He's not. He's had arthritis in his back and legs for years."

"Of course. I'm so sorry to hear that. A friend is an important asset."

Henry's lips twitched at the word *asset.* He leaned in and patted Jasper's head. "I got him after my wife died."

The lady nodded.

After Jessie died, he'd shut himself off, let the mail pile up and the answering machine collect condolences. Until one day, the boys had had enough and used his spare key, told him to get himself together. They weren't going to let their friend waste away. Told him he ought to get on one of those new internet dating services, plenty of good women still out there. Not like Jess, no. But a man needed company. He'd gone that afternoon to the SPCA and chosen Jasper. The other dogs had jumped and nipped at the bars, but the old lab had sat there waiting like a stoic soldier for Henry's decision. He'd thumped his tail against the concrete floor when Henry whispered, *You're the one.*

The lady scratched behind the old dog's ears, then stood in silence, her breath visible between them in the crisp air. Henry got the feeling she wanted to tell him something. She kept glancing up at him then back at Jasper, then over to her house. In the end, she just turned and walked up her driveway, a couple plastic bags clutched over her heart like they were made of Kevlar.

That night Jasper dragged himself to the door, his hind legs dangling useless. Henry lifted him, carried him out to the bitter cold night. He set him in the brittle grass and held all the dog's weight in the harness strap while Jasper wobbled on his front paws. Henry strained his neck back to watch the indifferent sky until the moment passed. He carried him inside, laid him beside his own bed, reaching down when Jasper's whimpers woke him during the night. In the morning, the whimpering had turned into a low howl-like moan that felt vaguely famil-iar to Henry, like ancestry or forgotten kisses. When Henry rubbed his head, the lab's entire body clenched. Big brown eyes searched Henry's, pleading with Henry to give him what he needed. It was the same imploring look Jessie had given him that last month. Too many needles, pinched smiles, plastic lines of hopeful poison—too much frustrated rest. At least this time he had a choice. All he had to do was tell the vet they were ready. Hold his friend, so Jasper's letting go could be a bit easier. Hold him like he had held Jess all those years ago. *Goddammit.* Henry snatched his keys.

The next six days blurred by like soldiers in formation, with a silence so loud it kept Henry awake, wandering the empty rooms like a ghost desperately seeking someone to haunt. After he gathered Jasper's ashes from the vet, sleep claimed him for three more days, until he woke on the tenth day to the pops of gunfire and the scent of jasmine. Henry rubbed the heels of his hands against his eyes, brushed away lingering dream fragments of bloodied hands in desert sands holding small, tight flowers.

He stared at the bare floor beside the front door while he tied his walking shoes. Without Jasper, Henry felt exposed, like he had put down a revolver or bulletproof vest instead of an old dog.

The lady's forehead wrinkled when she saw Henry walking alone. As he came closer, the wrinkles smoothed like running a hand over a sheet while making a bed. She grasped his hand, which ached from its missing weight, and squeezed gently. Her lips moved. It took Henry a minute to silence the artillery in his head. She was talking about her son. An army sergeant who had gone missing in Afghanistan. Henry remembered a news story a couple years back about a local man with a mother still in the area. Yellow ribbons had marked mailboxes and trees in the neighborhood, but he'd never really paid much attention. Another tragedy. Another yearning. And over time the ribbons had frayed and disappeared. She confided that she'd converted her son's room into a basic laboratory, taught herself from the internet and a willing professor how to process DNA samples. She'd thrown her life savings into buying expensive equipment. Said she was looking for reasons, for culprits, for answers—for him.

Later, she will show Henry her missing son's room. He will see the tall metal racks containing trays of glass slides and test tubes, flinch when they rattle against his touch. But now, she is looking at Henry with wide, sharing eyes, not so different than his own, and he returns her squeeze with the hand she still holds.

"What's your name?" Henry croaks out, his throat dry.

"Kameko."

Henry nods. "Pretty. What does it mean?"

"Turtle child."

Henry grins. "I thought you were gonna say flower." They walk along her ditch, patrolling it together. He kneels down to retrieve a cigarette butt, hands it up to her on his palm like a flag offered.

HOW TO CROSS THE STREET WITHOUT DYING

Her high-tops hopscotch between outstretched arms and legs, trying not to let dirty soles touch faded white limbs. Chalk outlines of neighborhood boys who fell in motion. White stains on pavement, like a pictorial teaching kids how to cross a street. On her way home from school, they are upside down, like krumpers* on heads, legs waving good-bye.

A reporter stands on the corner and speaks into a camera about robbing youth. The neighborhood's abuzz with the news of crimes that happen after dark. Old ladies scuttle onto flaking porches and *tsk-tsk* when they see her walk by. Poppop says, *He fell first.* She's not sure if he means that he's the first chalk outline on her way to school, or if she's next.

She's got no one to ask. She only has Poppop's word for it and the empty top bunk for the last four nights. The other two are names that flit about the older kids' conversations, the ones who skid off when they see Marco's little sister coming. She matches the echoed names to a freckled-bridge nose crinkled at an off-color joke, and the other, just the phrase, *Tell your little sister to fuck off,* under dark shades and flip-backed cap.

Everybody repeats, *He fell into the wrong crowd.* Wrong crowd.

---

*Krumping is an urban dance style, often an outlet for anger and alternative to street violence.

Wrong crowd. Like it was a choice on a multiple-answer test. Like Marco should have turned his pencil over to erase the darkened bubble, picked again.

Every time they cross over, her friend, Cherrie, says *Don't look down,* like they're walking a tightrope. She places feet carefully, never looks up. Her gaze retraces the three boys, searching for any detail in the scribble to determine how she's related. She reads the dead, deciphers their lesson on how to cross the street without dying.

THE LONG ROAD

The rainy season had carpeted the Zambian flood plain with opportunistic cattle, and the one road to Mongu bisected it like an American football touchdown line. What Billie wanted most in his life was waiting for him at the end of that road, but the fifty-nine miles might as well have been edged with college linebackers, for as easy as it was going to be for him to reach his goal. A beat-up sedan rusted brown came barreling by him, spewing gravel on his bare legs, then slowed down.

"Hey, Billie! Coming to school today?" A dark boy with white teeth yelled out the driver's side window, arm hanging out and slapping the door for emphasis.

"Nah, man. He's got too many house chores to do," the boy in the passenger seat replied.

Laughter and dust from the only car in town choked the lone boy walking as it sped off toward the low-slung cement block building the village called school. The weight of the two plastic jugs of water he carried on his shoulders gave him a backache, but he gritted his teeth and kept walking, determined to keep his balance. His father expected those jugs before breakfast.

Billie grunted as he dropped the containers beside his family's mud hut alongside the road, the only road from his village of Senanga to the capital city of Western Province, Mongu. Travelers were few; luckily for them it was the start of the dry season and the likelihood of getting bogged down in mud was low, but they'd have to watch for the pocked-out areas that dotted this stretch like the spots on the leopards in Kafue National Park.

Mizanda came around the back of the hut and acknowledged his son with a low grunt. "Only two jugs? You'll have to fetch more at noontime."

"Da, I have school. It's review for the English testing," Billie said. When his father did not respond, he added, "It's important, Da."

"Water isn't?"

"Da, please. Can it wait till suppertime? I'll get twice as much then."

"What's more important, to respect your father's wishes, or your English review?"

Billie looked down at the black soil, cracked dry at his father's feet. "I'll get it now, Da," he said as he turned to start the trek back to the handprint water tower that had been there since he was born. The squat tower sat in a field beside the Zambezi River, marked with foreign hands in red, white, and blue paint. He reached up and placed his palm against the blue one marked *Billie* in another's print, mirroring it like a twin.

He wondered again about the Billie on the water tower. His mom never spoke of him, and his father never talked of anything but how many chores needed to get done with a sick wife and only one son. He walked fast to get to school, but he was still late. Students crammed the dusty room, ranging in age from five to Billie and his colleagues, who were the oldest at fifteen. Now it was time for them to either get funding from the mission for American college or figure out a way to scrape by in this community.

Their teacher, Mr. Thomas, clapped his hands to get everyone's attention.

"For those of you going to Mongu for your college testing, there's been a problem with the mission director driving here tomorrow."

Billie looked up quickly. Mr. Thomas pushed his wire-rimmed eyeglasses up the bridge of his nose with a chalky finger and continued, "Clive has offered to drive you boys to the testing center. You still need to meet here at two p.m. tomorrow."

Billie turned to look at Clive, the boy whose family owned the only car in Senanga. He was grinning back at Billie, who closed his eyes and clutched his hand over his stomach.

The day passed quickly, concentrating on reviewing for the test that could get him in a real university. If he did badly on that test, it really didn't matter what Clive and his cronies did to him. He'd be stuck in the endless loop to fetch water for the remainder of his life, like a noose that tightened but never snapped. When Mr. Thomas tapped his fingers on the paper Billie was hunched over, he looked up questioningly.

"Yes, sir?"

"Go home, Billie. You can't cram any more into your head today. Go sleep on it."

"Yes, sir."

The hut was darkening with the evening sky. A long shadow fell across the floor as he stood in the open doorway. His mom was lying on her pallet in the center of the circular room. Her complexion was darker than Billie's, yet he noticed how pale she had become since the last dry season. She struggled with a smile as her son entered the one-room hut, reaching out her hand for him to grasp.

"My boy," she said in her soft voice and he wondered, if she hadn't been sick for so long, if her voice would be different, if she would be different.

"Mama."

She closed her eyes, and for a moment he thought she might slip away, but she just stretched her smile and whispered, "Love you, boy."

They sat for a few minutes. When the silence started asking questions, he spoke the most persistent one. "Mama, why did you name me after the man named Billie on the handprint tower?"

Her breath came slow and even and he thought perhaps she had drifted off to sleep, but then she spoke, and when she spoke her voice sounded like the one he imagined earlier she might have without her sickness. "We have to have hope."

It wasn't exactly the answer he was searching for, but it was a more concrete answer to that question than she had ever given, and so he sat in contemplation while he rubbed her hand in his two that had grown larger than hers.

"And, I love you, boy."

"I love you too, Mama."

The next morning Billie made three trips to the handprint tower, ensuring his parents would have plenty of water until his return the next day from Mongu. He tended the fire pit, mashed the maize meal and added it to boil for the nashima paste that would last several meals. He roasted some tubers in peanut powder and cayenne pepper for chinaka, his father's favorite dish. He swept the dirt floor in the hut and yard.

Finally, it was time to walk to the school for the long ride to the testing center. His mother had fallen asleep on her pallet and he kissed her gently on her forehead, something she would not have allowed had she been awake, even though the missionaries had said this would not contaminate Billie with her illness.

"So you are off then." Mizanda appeared beside the entrance to the hut, as if summoned by Billie's illicit touch.

Billie looked at the dusty feet of his father. "Yes, sir."

"Testing won't get your mother's meals made."

His father stared at Billie like he could pin him to the spot with his glare. The rattle of Clive's car passing by on the way to the schoolyard jolted Billie into his first step past his father. "I have to go, Da."

His father didn't answer as Billie stepped past him and started jogging down the road toward town, fearful that he would call him back and forbid him to go, even when he was far enough away that the river drowned out all other noise. He could see his colleagues gathering around Clive's car, with him still in the driver's seat, like a king on the village's only throne.

"There he is. The *boy* we've been waiting for." Clive made the word *boy* a slur.

"Okay, boys. Listen, it's about a three-hour drive to Mongu. Most of the major washouts have been patched up, but the ruts can still get pretty deep. Take your time. You should get there in plenty of time for a decent night's sleep at the mission before the testing tomorrow morning." Mr. Thomas gave each of the boys a hearty pat on the shoulder for good luck, except Clive, who never got out of the car.

"Yah, yah. Boys, let's get in and get on with it then," he yelled from the driver's seat.

They finished a hasty good-bye and scrambled into the vehicle. Shadrick claimed his regular spot beside Clive. Melo and Sonkwe pushed each other over the bench seat in the back, making room for Billie, who slid in last. They shot out of the schoolyard with a stuttering clutch, waving to the children that ran behind them through the yard and down the main road until they passed the last hut. Clive pushed his foot to the metal floorboard, causing the car to lurch forward with a burst of speed not unlike the cheetahs that sometimes attacked the stragglers of the cattle herds that moved in for the grasses that sprouted after the wet season.

"Hey, house boy, you think you're gonna do better on the testing than me?" Clive asked, staring at Billie in the cracked rearview mirror. "You think you're going to college?"

Shadrick chorused, "Yah, you think you're going to America? Your poppa has too many house chores for you to do. Maybe you should buy a dress in Mongu to wear while you carry water and mash cornmeal." Shadrick laughed and punched Clive on the shoulder. Melo chuckled softly into his hand in the back seat while Sonkwe sat with eyes wide, looking back and forth between the front seat and Billie sitting beside him.

Billie looked out the side window at the dusty road beside the Zambezi River, the only landscape he, and his father before him, had ever known. He wished he could bottle up the boys' words and throw them out the window into the waiting rush of the river, have them ride its current all the way down to Victoria Falls where they would shatter apart as they descended into Mosi-oa-Tunya, *the smoke that thunders*, forming new phrases, new meanings.

"You know what I think, Shadrick," Clive said, still staring at Billie. "I think Billie *boy* here doesn't understand that he's not as smart as he thinks he is."

Clive switched his glare to Melo. "Melo, who's got the car?"

"You do, Clive." Melo stole a contrite sideways glance at Billie.

"That's right. I knew you were a smart one, Melo. Maybe you'll make it to college with me and Shadrick."

The tip of Clive's tongue darted over his dry lips. "How about you, Sonkwe? You starting to feel a little crowded back there?" Clive stomped on the brake pedal and skidded to a stop so suddenly Shadrick's head made a dull thudding noise on the dash and Sonkwe half fell into the front seat.

"Hey, Sonkwe, I know it's crammed back there, but you have to stay in the back," Clive said as he shoved the other boy back roughly.

"Out." Clive motioned to the door with a swift jerk of his head, looking at Billie.

"But, Clive, it's like fifty-four more miles to Mongu," Shadrick said, laughing nervously.

"Well, somebody's getting out of the car. Use your brain, Shadrick. How many scholarships you think they give to Senanga boys?" He looked at each of them in turn. "Any of you want to take house boy's place and walk to Mongu?" They cast their eyes to their laps. Billie grabbed his small sack that contained a clean shirt, small cake of soap, bit of nashima, and a dog-eared toothbrush.

"No, man, you'll be leaving that." Clive's voice had gone low and dangerous. Billie recognized it as the voice he reserved for private meetings behind the school building, when Billie would leave with bruises under faded cotton. His face burned as he dropped the sack and stood back from the car.

"Sonkwe, make yourself useful and shut the door," Clive said. Sonkwe looked at the door handle as he pulled it shut.

"Hey, Billie! Why don't you just swim to America? The ocean's that way." Clive pointed out the window as he jolted off, leaving Billie in a cloud of dust and misery.

He looked to his left and saw the five miles back to his village. He looked to his right and saw the fifty-four miles to Mongu. In front of him was the Zambezi River, diminished from the overabundance of a month ago, shrunken back to a tamed flow. Behind him was the vast plain of grasses, which were starting their annual drying up, mirroring the Zambezi. He looked down at his two feet. Fifty-four miles. Could he make it in time for the testing tomorrow morning at seven o'clock? The weight of his father pulled at him to turn back and walk the easy distance to his hut and his familial responsibilities—as he turned in the direction of Mongu.

All that afternoon he jogged. When he got thirsty he drank from the banks of the river, watching for crocodiles and giving the hippopotamuses a wide berth. He scanned the horizon for big cats, having grown up with horror stories about predator attacks on humans. Yet, still he jogged until he had to walk. The treetops carried the sun when he reached the marker post that told him he had thirty-five more miles to Mongu. Billie's legs ached, but he pushed on another hour in dusk.

When the dark overcame him, he allowed himself a rest and stretched out on the gravel. He didn't dare leave the road now, as he couldn't be assured that he would be able to find his way back to it in the black. The growl of a big cat startled him awake. He got up and started walking, the crunch of gravel under tennis shoes the only indicator that he was staying on his path. Animal sounds punctuated the darkness: hippos trumpeting, hyenas cackling, grass owls screeching, leopards growling. At one point, he thought he heard his father calling him back all the many miles to his village. By dawn, with the rising sun,

Billie saw another milepost in the distance. He had ten more miles to walk. He sunk to his knees and sobbed, his hands trembling as they rubbed his weary face. *We have to have hope.* His mother's voice, carried on a warm wind, brushed his ear. He groaned and gingerly stood, walked to the riverbank to splash cool water on his face and arms, reviving himself enough to continue his journey.

The sun was above the collection of buildings that sprung up from the road when he finally reached Mongu. Every part of his body cried, but he didn't have the energy to weep. He knew the testing center from Mr. Thomas's descriptions and he walked in. Clive, Shadrick, Melo, and Sonkwe sat in the first row with a few other boys their age behind them. They looked clean, rested, fed, and surprised.

Billie turned his focus on the administrator who walked from the front of the room to the door where Billie stood.

"Yes?"

"I'm here for the testing. My name is on the list."

The administrator's eyes had a familiar glint as he said, "You want to take the test? That'll be twenty-five thousand kwacha."

"The testing has already been paid for by the mission."

"Oh, you're right. But the pencil to take the test will be twenty-five thousand kwacha."

Billie searched the desks of his comrades, ignoring Clive's sniggering from his seat. There were three pencils in front of Clive, freshly sharpened. The others had two and when Melo went to reach one of his out to Billie, Clive shot him a murderous glance and gave a minute shake of his head. Melo placed the pencil carefully back.

Billie abruptly turned and walked outside. His mind raced in circles. How was he going to take that test? He had to take that test. Should he go to the mission and ask for more money? The mission was across the city, and he needed to be taking the test now. It was a timed test and he was already late. He frantically scanned the street, taking in the pedestrians and vendors hawking their wares: dried fish, tubers, hats, cheap sunglasses.

He looked down at his dusty fatigued body. He had nothing to sell. Except maybe his tennis shoes, which were already thirdhand when he got them, but they were still, even with his long journey, better than most of the homemade shoes many people wore. He quickly bent and pulled them off, waving them in the air and frantically calling for a buyer. Twenty-five thousand kwacha was expensive for a pencil. Twenty-five thousand kwacha was cheap for a pair of shoes.

A woman with a shrewd look snatched them up and didn't even bother to haggle with Billie over the price, scurrying off with her bundle clutched to her chest as if he might run after her and grab them back.

Billie handed the money to the administrator and took his pencil and test. The next three hours Billie answered test questions like he was singing, like he was God and knew everything without struggle. He created mountains and valleys and aircraft with his answers. Clive could no longer torture him. His mother was no longer ill. His father understood.

When he finished the last question and looked up from the test, he saw that although he was the last one to start, he was the first one to finish. He turned the paper in to the administrator, who leveled him with an astonished gaze, and walked out of the building and back to the road. He looked to his left and saw the cluster of buildings that was Mongu. He looked to his right and saw the long devastating stretch of road to his village. He looked down at his bare feet, swollen and blistered from his horrendous night.

The weighty pull of the buildings called to him to seek solace in their shade as he started his long walk back to the village. He shrugged the weight off and continued. He knew he could make it. His journey was going to be longer than many people's he knew, but the distance didn't bother him anymore.

When a rusted brown sedan sputtered up to him, he did not slow down.

"Hey, man, get in the car," Clive shouted.

Billie kept walking, looking at the horizon.

"Don't be stupid, man, get in the car," Shadrick said.

Billie kept walking, looking at the horizon.

"I said get in the car," Clive bit out.

Billie stopped. He looked at Clive and the others in their forced vanity and said, "I would rather walk the road with the cheetahs than get in a car with a snake."

"It's a long way, man," Clive said, but he couldn't hide the quiet sound of admiration in his tone, or maybe, Billie thought, his ears were just hearing sharper than they had the day before.

BURNT WINGS

Julie started out in life two minutes behind Trevor, an after-thought like the nicked candles and Santa mugs from clearance bins, tissue paper hiding chipped rims. Items the kids on her route handed her while parents, whose names she didn't know, waved from the curb that week before winter break. With no kids of her own and a wrecked marriage, she'd crammed the seasonal offerings into her luggage and crashed at her brother's place one state over for the holiday. Awake all night, she'd filled the hours sipping tea from Santa's frontal lobe and watching green candles burn, occupied with past promises and projections on bare walls.

Trevor had sworn they'd talk. He just needed to drive by a friend's to score some holiday spirit. By the time the candles' shadows flickered from church arches to angel wings, she knew. The heavy tread outside apartment 312 was not going to be Trevor. The suffocating scent of balsam only pretended comfort, another halfhearted afterthought. The fake fir scent failed to disguise the spilt beer, bedsheets well past washing, and memories of teenage years. Years spent joking away her twin. When passing out in your car in the middle of your front yard could still be consid-ered a joke. The car he'd bought cheap by mowing middle-aged neighbors' lawns. Smart enough to take his shirt off when the front curtains fluttered.

Julie scraped out a laugh, choking the flames to falter back and forth. *Middle-aged.* Had she turned into ghostly fluttering behind curtains, too? How many nights had she waited up for her brother's return? Worry etched her face long before the years could stake that claim. Like candles in the dead of the night, she knew his luck would eventually sputter out.

Before the muffled clearing of a stranger's throat, the flickering wings of shadows stretched long, like they might touch heaven if she'd just let them keep trying. When the knock finally came, she pinched charred wicks, allowing the burning to die. It didn't exactly hurt, but the flames left black that smeared everything she touched.

HEART INSURANCE

As Henry James trudged the four miles along city streets to his apartment on the lower east side, his thoughts spiraled low, like the hopes of his clients he'd been on the phone with all day. The ones he inevitably told were not on the *Noteworthy* list, therefore not eligible to receive coverage for the diseases that plagued them. A statement that would no doubt be read to him one day, considering his genetic propensity for cardiomyopathy. At forty-nine percent on his Death Pie chart, the most likely thing to kill him. That wedge in his chart was the reason he'd taken the position of Insurance Regulator at Mayflower Industries in the first place, to acquire the one benefit that mattered from the menial job—the overwrite code. One day, all those years blabbering into the phones with dying people would finally come to fruition.

A pile of street thugs clotted the sidewalk up ahead, and Henry ducked into a corner grocer for a pack of hot dogs and a carton of milk. The aisles were crammed with bright packages that flickered in the fluorescent lights as he ambled over to the meat locker on the back wall and punched in his private code for access to the packages of gluten-free hot dogs, free-range pigeon patties, and pigeon patty substitutes. He grabbed a hot dog pack, then headed up front where the milk cartons were open to the public on a shelf near the check-out. West Highland

terriers grinned from the cartons, and he wondered, not for the
first time, if they really utilized the small breed for milk production or if it was just a marketing ploy since the dogs were
white and cute and not very intimidating. *Savvy advertising* was
running through his brain at the exact moment the clerk fired
his simulator gun at a young thief shoving comic books under
his shirt. The clerk was dead-on and the boy lay convulsing in
rhythmic fashion on the linoleum, causing Henry to notice the
cracks radiating across the floor like spider veins in old calves.
The thin synthetic line, still attached to the dart embedded in
the twitching boy, twittered all the way up to the cash register,
where the clerk propped the gun against a display of cigarette
lighters shaped like naked women.

Henry placed his items on the counter and the clerk rang him
up. He fished out his credit card, emblazoned with his Death Pie,
a new design gifted to all employees as a holiday bonus. Mayflower
Industries wanted their employees and clients to be aware of their
choices when impulse buying—you couldn't say they didn't warn
you. The wiser choice might have been the pigeon patty substitute
made with ingredients Henry couldn't pronounce, held together
with corn syrup and artificial flavoring, but sometimes you had
to splurge. You just couldn't fake the taste of meat.

The clerk swiped Henry's card.

"That's the new Painful Death simulator?" Henry bobbed his
hand toward the gun.

"Yeah, newest model. Came in last week. The neighborhood
ain't what it used to be." He nodded toward the kid, who jerked in
a pattern not unlike the dances Henry sometimes tried to emulate
on *Dance, Dance TV* Saturday nights after he'd allowed himself
a half carafe of red wine to narrow his chance of clogged carotid

arteries by nineteen percent. Henry envied the kid's rhythm, then turned back to the clerk, took his card and grabbed the bag, stepping over the line still quivering from the dart embedded in the kid's thrashing thigh.

"Thanks." Henry nodded to the clerk.

"Have a good one."

The street thugs had gone, leaving the sidewalk clear except for a skittering scrap of purple hair, little pieces of scalp holding the blowing strands together so that it looked like a stray animal scurrying toward the gutter grate. A splattering of blood trailed off behind an alley dumpster. The distant sound, *hout, hout, hout,* of the thugs' initiation carried over the metallic rush of buses. Automatic doors swooshed open as Henry passed, slogans loudly chanted from speakers with fake trademarked enthusiasm.

Henry knew he could get hit by a bus or shot in a random act of violence, but statistically at three and sixteen percent, he felt pretty good about his chances. Plus he took pedestrian safety and his yearly Bystander-Risk Reduction class very seriously. Sometimes he was curious about what *other—1%* might entail, though he figured it was a catchall to cover the company's liability. Ironically, the second highest score on his Death Pie was suicide at thirty-one percent, but he felt like he had that under control. Although lately, in the middle of certain calls, when a woman was droning on and on about her child's potential for success, how her six-year-old had woken up with a runny nose on test day, how if she had known he would be in that rare four percent of people who developed leukemia as adolescents she'd have appealed the Potentiality Test score for him that very day he entered kindergarten instead of begging with an insurance regulator on the phone a half dozen years later, how if Henry could just press the acceptance button…in the middle of *those* calls, he sometimes imagined climbing the fire stairwell to roof access and jumping off, past the lush vice presidents' offices on the top floor, past Jeannette in receiving, past his own cubicle window, to land with a solid splat on the sidewalk below. Making a space, an outline of his body, through the crowd. Something that said, *Henry was here*, like graffiti or a heart cut into a tree. Maybe his landing would be so fierce the cement would crack, causing all current and future employees of Mayflower Industries to point and say, *That's where Henry the Regulator died*, a warning symbol or at least a conversation starter. In any event, he hoped his disease would pop up soon, so he could do the override and quit his job to become a fire technician like he'd always wanted.

Henry passed Fire Station No. 537 and climbed the seven flights to his bachelor apartment. His building, a former tenement listed on the Historic Register, was a national treasure that now leaned a bit to the left. The top floor was toppling over itself into tiny pieces of rubble that sometimes struck Henry on his shoulders like a tap of recognition. His ceiling leaked when the people upstairs bathed their Siberian huskies, and the only window had a cracked sill that blew frigid air in the winter, freezing him while he boiled hot dogs on the rusty stove. Even so, the main selling point of the apartment had been the outstanding view from that window of High Electric Logistical Park. Its wires upon wires stretching from heavy metal poles, like Atlas rotted down to sinews, holding the world in place. Tonight was a Tuesday, so Henry unwrapped his package of hot dogs and tossed three in a pot to boil. He stuck the milk in his mini fridge and wandered over to the window to peer at the kites flying. Teenagers frequented the park. They had death matches, placed bets on the lightweight metallic kites especially made to dart through the wires. They were sharply detailed with fanciful designs of tiny skulls and crossbones in shades of sunset. Most were shaped like dragons or Jesus or pop singers, but sometimes a remarkably extravagant one would veer by his window, an entire manga episode depicted in its folds.

Henry crossed back to the stovetop, stabbed the pink dogs with a fork as they bobbed in the boil like fish in a bucket, reminding him of when they had been actually made of mackerel. When he was a kid and the hot dogs had that slick oily taste that made them practically slide down your throat, left a light film on your lips that lingered till bedtime. Before the fish dried up and after the larger animals became too hard to maintain with all the acres of grain feed shriveled to dust. Before the manufacturers made the switch to real canines for the meat byproduct. The obvious choice, really, when you thought about it, although they didn't like to advertise the fact. Customers demanded meat. You just couldn't fake the taste of meat.

Red, orange, and yellow flashes lit the muted kitchen. At least once a week, one of the kites got blown into the wires and hung there tangled while great sparks shot through black sky, like on extra boring days at work when Henry cooked tinfoil in the microwave. Henry glanced toward the window. The standby medics scrambled over and nudged the body, still gripping the kite wire, with their long rubber poles until the sparking and twitching stopped. Then they carried it over to the kite slide, a long covered tube at the edge of the park that was rumored to end at the production line of the meatpacking plant. Hence the saying you often heard when walking past playground fences,

Stupid meathead! You're gonna ride the kite slide. Henry didn't
think it'd be a good way to go, but he guessed that was where
the thrill came in.

There had once been a girl who'd made his existence full of
sparks, like the metallic kites lighting up the night. But Henry
had buried her long ago in passed minutes and excuses and boiled
hot dogs on Tuesday nights. She had wanted him to move to the
West Coast with her, but that would have meant quitting his
job at Mayflower before his cardiomyopathy popped up and he
could do the overwrite. It wasn't the reasonable thing to do. So
he had quietly said *no* and shooed her away. She sent postcards,
randomly, for a few months after she left. The last one was from
Death Valley, California, ducks swimming in a line across Bad-
water Basin. She wrote, *See? Your ducks could get their act together
here, too.* Then she had added, *with me,* and a pathetic string of
x's and *o*'s that trailed off at the bottom corner under his address
that she'd written by heart.

He had taped the ducks to his mini fridge, opposite the view
of the electrical park. Each week when the sparks flew, they
reflected on the glossy paper, making the ducks swim across
rainbows. He tapped it now with his finger, bent in and lifted
the bottom to see the script on the back. The postmark was
seven years ago.

Sirens blared, not the sharp kind when a store's alarm has been
tripped, or even the whirly wails of the kite park—but a rusty hack,
like an old man coughing. It took a second for Henry to realize
the dusty caps in the hallway of his tenement had come alive with
effort. He smoothed the postcard down flat and shuffled over to
the door, hesitating a moment before cracking it. A thick gray
wall billowed into his apartment. The building wasn't to safety

code, didn't have to be since it was on the Historic Register. Of course the lease contained extra clauses. Ones that informed it was each resident's responsibility to obtain their own personal foam-protection ball with air pockets, recommendation three hours and up to 1,451 degrees Fahrenheit. However, fire did not occupy a wedge on Henry's chart, and so it had not occurred to him to bother with the legalese of foam protection.

The neighbors liked to smoke hatchem and hallucinate about floating on mega yachts, fucking Siberian teenage models in Swiss Miss pudding, while actually just lying facedown on the carpet. Henry once ran into a pod of them at the mailbox stand. The smallest, with green stripes in her hair, had told him about the smoking and pudding. She had carpet imprint on her cheek, crinkles with dingy shag strands sticking out like a child trying on a pretend beard. Henry figured their recreational pastime was the most probable reason for the gray cloud hovering in his apartment. It smelled like how he imagined day-old popcorn and lint might taste. He envisioned the girl with green stripes' forehead melting into mottled carpet.

A barrier of flames engulfed the hall. Henry walked back to his kitchen and shoved the window up, contemplated the view. If he had his druthers he'd jump clear across to the electrical wires, tiptoe along like a rubber gymnast invulnerable to the charge, shimmy down the pole and triple Salchow to stick the landing. But even now, with the heat licking his temples, competing with the tepid breeze, he knew that was an impossible feat.

He glanced back at the postcard from that girl, the one who still mattered. The edge fluttered in the intense heat, like it was a heart trying to tear itself free. He wondered what the girl was doing at that very moment and pictured her standing over a boiling pot of pink dogs, looking at the only letter he'd written her. But he knew the probability of that was approaching zero. Since she never cared for the taste of meat and he had never written her, although he wished he were the type of man that would have.

And then, like seven years ago, he had to decide whether to jump or to burn.

GIRAFFES

The girl's mom let Jason out at the curb.
His first official date, Nacho Night at a youth group, over.
"How was it?" I asked, wiping dried cheese off his white
button-up. He batted my hand away, grabbed an applesauce
from the pantry.
"The preacher talked about *it*. He said God made sex and it
was good."
"The preacher said that?"
"Yah. God told John that sex was good."
"John the Baptist?"
"I don't know. God told everybody sex was good."
"I thought it was supposed to be Nacho Night."
"We played trivia to get our nachos. Dolphins have sex for fun.
Most giraffes are bisexual because they have teeny brains."
"I could of went without knowing that."
He shrugged.
"God, Jason, weren't you embarrassed?"
"A little when the film started."
"What'd you do?"
"We ate nachos."
"I'm not sure you're seeing this girl again."
"Why?"
"Because she invites you to sex lessons at church."

"I really like that church. It was fun."

I told him to finish his applesauce and go to bed. Frankly, I'll never look at giraffes the same again.

TREADING WATER

Mark is being torn in two. A girl with dark curls winks at him as she pulls the jagged teeth of the magician's saw across his chest. The crowd oohs and ahhs. *Bite down on this. It'll only hurt for a second.* She grins for the audience. Laughter from the dark theater morphs into a low roar of applause that awakens his thirst. He's forgotten his part in the act. The spotlight blinds him. There is something he needs to remember. The roar grows louder, pinpointed directly overhead, blocking out the glaring light.

Mark's hand jerks to his chest. He pries crusty eyes open and recognizes the spin of blades hovering. A helicopter. The burning across his chest not a sideshow act, but the man-of-war that grazed him before he climbed onto the particleboard, cheap-ass door that saved his life.

Tanshe—tropical paradise, the ad had claimed. *A second chance for a new beginning*, Adam had proclaimed, with enough certainty that Mark had fooled himself into believing, too. Until it wasn't— paradise. Adam still whined. The poolside service was slow. The eggs Benedict had been better at the resort in Key West. How handsome the waiter was, and don't think he didn't notice Mark looking. How he'd had it. He wasn't going to deal with another Robert situation. A commitment was a commitment.

Mark had barked at Adam, if he'd wanted a nagging wife he'd

have stayed in the closet. He'd clenched his jaw, grabbed the room key, and headed back up the two flights to their room. Stretching his stride, taking the steps two at a time, feeling his frustration in the burn of his thighs. Until he was far enough away from Adam's complaints, but not high enough to escape the tsunami when it hit.

On his second switchback on the outside stairwell, he'd noticed the beach dotted with people waving their arms as yellow specks blurred into the horizon. He was embarrassed that his first instinct was to watch in morbid curiosity. He did not think of Adam still lounging at the poolside buffet, waiting for his mimosa to be served by the attractive, but admittedly slow waiter. He did not think about being the stronger swimmer. About how, only yesterday, he'd laughed at Adam's doggy paddle to the resort's swim-up bar.

What did cross his mind was how the wave headed toward them sounded not unlike the emaciated lion in the traveling circus that came to his hometown once when he was eight. How his teacher had declared, *We may never get another chance,* and talked the principal into a field trip. How, at the cages before the show, Mark had tempted the wearied beast with a bit of candy apple to dazzle a classmate. How it had eaten out of his hand. How unimpressed he had been, later, as he watched the lion tamer's performance from the bleachers.

When the wave came, his first instinct was to watch in morbid curiosity, then clamp the keycard between his teeth, free flailing limbs to keep above water. Useless. Like he still needed a key, a room. The ocean had taken over. Doors of the ocean-side hotels ripped off their hinges to become riffraff to which Mark clung.

Now, a gurney swings from a line spindling down. The bitter taste of the keycard lingers on his tongue, cutting the dryness welling inside him. Ocean spray from the helicopter's rotary blades beats his chest. Part of him will be saved. Part of him has been treading water for years, is still treading water. Rescue hovers while loved ones drown.

AMERICAN HOLIDAY

My name's Amber Jones. It's Christmas and Ma's been locked up for twenty-seven days now. You may have heard of her, the BF Killer, she's sort of famous around here in Tucker, Mississippi. You think they could of come up with a cleverer nickname, but it's the holiday season and I guess even as worked up as they all are over what my mama did, everybody mostly just wants to take off and go home.

We live in a double-wide next to the new Walmart. People said location's everything when the Johnsons next door got half a million for their land and moved to Florida, while we just got a crappy view of the parking lot. Mama said it was unfortunate but that it'd work out good for Black Friday. Aunt Betsy and her still camped out for three hours once they saw the first car pull up.

This all started over shrimp and grits Thanksgiving morning, when Ma and Aunt Betsy discussed tactical operations while flipping through store mailers, like Black Friday shopping was an athletic sport. First pick was Walmart, of course, with the seventy-inch flat-screen deal and the laptop for fifty bucks. I guess it's a good thing they snagged the laptop, since that's what we're getting ready to Skype Ma on. Ma's big like me. Bigger than Aunt Betsy, so she got the shoving and grabbing job. Even though Aunt Betsy always smells like French fries, she just doesn't have the weight to handle black-and-blue Friday. She held cart-in-line duty while Ma darted straight to electronics.

So here we all are, Jennie, Megan, Daddy, and me, waiting to see Mama on the fifty-buck laptop. We invited Aunt Betsy over. She said it was just too sad and she's working double shifts anyway, through the holidays to have time off for Ma's trial.

Daddy gets the Skype session set up. The screen goes gray. We see our faces reflected back, like we've got our own reality TV show. Then there's Mama sitting there with her hair a little limper than usual. A bright red sweater with a family of teddy bears decorating a Christmas tree looks festive over her prison-issue orange jumpsuit. She leans forward when she sees us, and the little jingle bells tinkle on her tree sweater.

We sit for a second and then Mama starts exclaiming about how nice everybody looks and how jail food's not as bad as all the movies make it out to be. Daddy says, "Honey, I'm driving down to Hopewell tomorrow for visiting hours."

She kind of clears her throat and tells everybody, "What are you waiting for? Open up those presents!"

Jennie tears into hers. She's already figured it out. It's a new cell phone. Only it's last year's model. Mama only grabbed one of the latest versions. And we all knew who'd get that. Jennie's okay with it though. At least now she's got voice command like everybody else. She makes a joke about her accent and how it'll never understand, like Megan in geometry.

Megan scowls at Jennie and sticks out her tongue. But only spares a second on her little sister, because her package is larger and she can guess what's inside. She jumps up and down when she sees the shiny silver icon on the white box. Ma tells her to settle down, she's jumping out of the video frame, but she's kind of laughing when she says it. Megan's in middle school now and the teachers let the kids use their tablets during class. Ma only snagged a mini this year, but it's a good transition to the full-size.

I'm up next. I know what I'm getting and it ain't tickets to the art museum in Birmingham like I asked for. Daddy's already opened his gift, of course. Otherwise we wouldn't be able to Skype Ma in jail. I had to wrap the presents, 'cause the cops were only about fifteen minutes behind Mama when she got home. Jennie and Megan sleep like dead cats, nothing wakes them up, but Daddy and I heard. We tried to stand up for her, but we hadn't been shopping. Mama was all frenzied up, red and splotchy like when she's drank too much of Grandma's Muscat wine, only she was just high on bargain buys. The older cop tried calming her down. The younger one kept holding his hands up and getting in her face. Mama said, "It wasn't even my fault! The bitch tried to snatch the last laptop right out my hands. All I did was shove her off of me."

People say it's all about location, location, location. It's unfortunate for my mama that the Tucker Walmart is only a twenty-minute drive from one of their largest distribution centers and had more than their fair share of flat screens for Black Friday. It's unfortunate for the lady she shoved, that she was standing directly in front of a precarious stack of Toshibas. I guess the lawyers will say it's the store's fault. Still, Mama thinks she's not coming home for a while.

Jennie's snapping selfies, making fishy faces that she think's sexy, but with her overbite, just makes her look like a donkey sucking on a lemon slice. Megan's reaching to plug in her present. Dad's fiddling with the contrast on the fifty-buck laptop. Ma's face is fading in and out while she peers through the screen, trying to find me in the middle of it all.

"Open your gift up," she's saying to me, like I'm not the one who wrapped it. "You can take it with you next year. Call me. I'll tell you what to get first." Yep. They say it's all about location. For me, I guess it's unfortunate I was born the oldest in this trailer, to this woman who's leaning into the camera, saying, "Somebody's got to carry on the family tradition."

DOG TIRED

Dammit. His mom was calling during the parade, again. The number one rule in the park was not to talk in costume. Dogs don't talk. Actually, that was number two. Number one was never take off your head in public, no matter what—claustrophobia, sweating, puking. Music blared from the float's speakers. It wasn't like anybody would hear him up here, above the screaming throng of snotty, dirty midgets. Not the real midgets, they were safely tucked inside their duck costumes two floats back.

Huey Campbell said, "Answer," into his headset, paws waving vigorously to the kids below. "Hey, Mom. It's the parade."

"It's always a parade. When are you coming home for Christmas?"

"It's not always a parade. They're at eleven thirty, three forty-five, and ten."

"And then there's photo time and magic time and every other type of time except call-your-mother time. There's never a *good time* to talk to you."

"Okay, Mom. I get it. What's up?"

Huey waved both paws. Turned and wagged his tail.

"I need to know when you're coming home. Penny's going to be here on the twenty-third with the kids."

"I can't make it. I have to work."

"You haven't been home for the holidays in years. Penny's kids are getting big. My only grandchildren."

Huey turned over his shoulder, spun around in little circles, chasing his dog tail.

"Mom. I have to work. You know that. Rick Flannogan has been drooling for my spot on the parade route for months. We're the same height category. The character opportunities in our size are extremely low."

"So let him have your spot and you come home for the holidays!"

"Mom! This dog gig is gold. I've worked hard for this. I'm limited. I'm too short for the prince rotation and too tall for the rodent population. It's either this, an action figure, or a friggin' chipmunk, Ma."

"Watch your mouth, Huey."

Huey was always watching his mouth. His view screen was the black mesh of the dog's mouth, a filter of gray. It gave everybody a kind of smoky look, a layer of ash after a volcano. He wasn't just a character, he was Mt. Vesuvius up here. Red dog tongue hanging like a lava flow.

"Just find a way to get home. I mean it. Rascal hasn't been doing that great. I think we're gonna lose him this year. His hind legs are giving out."

"Rascal? Really?"

"You're missing out, Huey. You get home. Bring a girl."

"Yah, Mom. I'll call you later."

Huey kept waving. December was his favorite time in the park. Decorations over the top, attendance at full capacity, it wasn't so stinkin' hot in the costumes, and he got paid overtime.

He blew a kiss to the crowd lined up, pushing against the roped sidewalks and each other. A little girl with pigtails sat on her daddy's shoulders, dug second-knuckle deep in her nostril. A ten-dollar chocolate banana had melted off the stick and matted in her father's hair. He looked like he might throw her into the floats.

Ringing in Huey's ear. *Seriously, another call? Great, Penny now.* He answered. Cut the pleasantries.

"I just talked to Mom. I'm not coming home."

"Huey, you have to come home. Mom's driving me nuts. It's not fair you stay down there and leave me here to deal with Mom and Dad. It's your turn. I can't handle another holiday where all Mom does is sit around and talk about how you aren't here. I want you to be here this time. See if she has anything else to say."

Huey grabbed his long black dog ears, covered his fake dog eyes.

"Penny, look, I'm going to lose my job if I fly to fuckin' Wisconsin in the middle of our high season. Just because you're tired of listening to Mom? Why don't you come down here? The kids would love it, and I could see you."

"Like last time? You saw them through the mesh in a dog's mouth. You friggin' denied it when I tried to explain it was you in there!"

"The number one rule is we're not allowed to give our identity away. I put the dog head on. I am the dog."

"Okay, whatever. You're getting weirder every year. Just come home."

A boy with large mouse hands smacked his younger brother in his stomach while the dad pointed at a brochure, argued with a red-faced woman. She looked like she wanted to grab the kid's mouse hands and punch the dad in the gut, too. Huey held his dog paws up, covered his dog mouth, his real eyes, slapped his canine thigh.

Penny was going on and on about gluten-free stuffing and something about Lucy getting married and having a kid.

"Whoa! Back up. What's this about Lucy having a kid? I just saw her. She was normal, same as always."

"You saw her four years ago. When you were home in February. She was at Aunt Remie's Super Bowl party and you were going to take her out the next day, but then that goofy-ass guy called and said he had a bulging disc and needed you to fly back to fill in."

"She's too young to have a kid. And it wasn't goofy, wrong height category. It was dumbo."

"She's thirty-three, Huey, just like you. We have biological clocks that go off at certain ages, you know."

"I don't know anything about clocks, but I just saw her and she didn't have a kid."

"Four years ago, Huey. Jeez. Just get home before the end of December."

"God, Penny. I've got to go. The parade's almost over. I get caught taking calls in this suit and I'm fired. Call you later."

"I mean it, Huey."

This was the part of the parade when the characters climbed off the floats and danced over to their designated signing locations. His spotter would prep the autograph books and pens so he could paw the signature, pose with the kids, ham it up for the cameras. The parents loved that shit. What did he need to fly all the way to friggin' Wisconsin for? To see a couple of nieces and nephews who he barely knew? Maybe run into some old girlfriend's little brats? Give all this up? He had kids lined up all the way to the goddamn castle waiting to hug him. No. His costume fit just right. He was the perfect size for it. And, he'd earned his spot.

DUST THERAPY

My dust is so deep, it has layers.
They go to group therapy on Thursday nights.
Slouch down on folding chairs in a circle,
discuss their fears of vacuums and glass
condensation. They speak condescendingly
about time and cohesive health-care plans.

Secretly, they scoff at dry rags and higher
education. They speak Spanish, and Italian,
too. Throw French phrases into conversations
when they want to appear worldly.

My dust mocks me behind soft hands. They
have a plan to conquer this house—then it's
just a matter of time before the lady next
door lets her guard down, and falls right
along beside me. While those cocky bunnies
giggle and wink. Climb over our corpses.

Insatiable bastards.

WONDER WOMAN IN SUBURBIA

Wonder Woman rang my bell, caught me peeping
between blind slats. She stood there looking all
shiny and smug on my front doorstep with her
snazzy lasso and ridiculous headband—an old-
fashioned dominatrix. You can't blame me for being
surprised, it was a sneak attack like Mormons
or vacation timeshare sales. Her invisible jet still
trailed steam, parked partially on my lawn, mailbox
knocked askew—kids' tricycles flattened.

Hands on hips. Then she pressed my button again,
clanged the brass knocker. *What the hell*, I said,
under my breath of course, and duly opened the
door (the kids napping amidst Legos on the living
room floor). *Come in. Come in. Glad you can grace
us with your presence.* I grinned. I wasn't worried,
Wonder Woman always mistook flattery for truth.

She pranced aloof through the foyer, declared she'd stay
for dinner. Did I have any wine? Maybe a gin and
tonic wasn't too much to ask? Tanqueray Ten, dash
of bitters on top. *Chop-chop!* She needed to relax after
all the burglaries she'd stopped and she'd adore a foot

massage, fighting criminals in heels was a serious
job. She felt underappreciated, sought a respite,
could I keep those kids quiet (awakened mid-nap,
they'd started to riot).

I slouched to the bar, pretended—clanked glasses
and ice, then just upended the tequila straight down
my throat, took my shot—bolted through the door,
jumped in the jet, smashed pedal to invisible floor,
guffawed at Wonder Woman's slack jaw on my
porch. Waved from the cockpit, mouthed, *I'll be
back—maybe.*

Let's see her super powers appreciate, lassoed to a
picket fence by three cranky kids.

ANDROMEDA ON THE STRANGENESS OF MEN*

My father advised me not to speak to strangers, then
stripped me naked, tied me to wet rocks. His hot
breath whispered it was harder for him than for me. One day
I'd understand….well, oops. Then he scurried over dunes
to watch at a safe distance.

I prayed in vain for a change of heart, then altered
my request to a fearless one (I consider myself a realist).
Miracle! Or universal coincidence if you don't subscribe
to religious thought. A man appeared in winged shoes
and halted mid-flight to ask, *Why? Why did your father chain
you to this rock?* As he gawked at breasts, armory
of a shaking heart, I spied the fiery dragon and held
my tongue, followed my old man's advice.

*According to Greek mythology, Andromeda was chained to rocks by her father
as a sacrifice to the sea monster that Poseidon unleashed when Andromeda's vain
mother boasted Andromeda was more beautiful than the Nereids. Perseus flew
by on Hermes's winged sandals after many adventures, including cutting off
Medusa's head and turning Atlas to stone to relieve his burden of shouldering
the weight of the world. Perseus battled the monster and saved Andromeda.
Later, they gave up their adventures, got married, and had children.*

ANDROMEDA LOOKS AT FIFTY

I am Andromeda already set free,
not ravished by the sea monster—
now drowning in our laundry.
Perseus transformed his wings into
minimum wage at the Blue Skyy
Vodka distillery, where he straightens labels,
tightens caps. On smoke breaks, he brags
about winged feet days, when cleverness
brought more than stony reflection. Most
Fridays, his boss lets him take an airplane
bottle home. Our children have grown lives
of their own. They pursued opportunity
to the West Coast. They post photos on
Facebook, expect us to boast to neighbors,
Our grandkids are beautiful beyond worlds.

I guess life's turned out…
the way it's supposed to be.
I go to a women's counselor
every Wednesday morning.
We discuss daddy issues
and the sacrifice of mothers.
Most nights Perseus doesn't

sleep well, his recurring dream
being stuck in Hades's helm*,
made invisible to the world.
The government named it post-
traumatic stress disorder, express
mails a check each month
that he's too embarrassed to cash.
So, he dresses in collared shirts
and practical shoes, pops
Nicorette gum, wobbles precariously
on his moped along the edge,
yellow-lined freeway to the spirit
factory, while I sit here mindlessly
watch TV, fold lukewarm laundry,
pen grocery lists, rinse breakfast dishes,
pour another coffee mug full—daydream
being back on slippery rocks,
chained to mythicized fate,
fantasize a dragon devouring youth.

*Perseus used Hades's helm, a cap that turns the wearer invisible, to vanquish
Medusa.

A CONVERSATION WITH ANDROMEDA
AT THE ASSISTED LIVING FACILITY

Perseus did not slay my dragon. Atlas should have stilled
the world from turning. I've been transformed into the sea
dragon my father bade me greet. You need proof? Notice
my dragon-scale skin, how the spots blend into another color
that I have never been. The white puffs of hair curls wisp
about my head, like smoke trace from faded breath. My
knotted bones and coiled veins lie on my skin like reptiles
sunning. The ultimate proof, of course, you won't see—my
dragon heart cooled inside my chest of treasured memory.

TO-DO LIST

Sophie was crying again. *Shut up*, popped into Billie's head, causing her to feel like the worst mother on the planet for at least the fifth time that morning.

"Dammit." She quickly rinsed the remainder of the shampoo out of her hair. A small hand yanked the shower curtain back. Billie gasped at the blast of cold air that tagged along with the pint-sized intruder. Nathan gripped the plastic curtain and wobbled. *Crap*, she had forgotten to lock the door.

"So So."

"Hey, sweetie. I know Sophie's upset. I can hear her all the way in here, but Mommy's a little busy right now. Where's Daddy?" She wrestled the curtain away from her son. Gave him the almost empty shampoo bottle to play with. "Michael," she yelled, as she turned off the water and reached for a towel.

Michael came to the open door. He already had his suit on and was straightening his navy tie. "You need to pick up the dry cleaning. This is my last clean shirt."

"You remember you're taking the kids to preschool, so I can get to my presentation? And what is wrong with Sophie?"

"Your presentation?"

"Yeah. The one I've been staying up late to finish for the past two weeks. The one I'm giving to the largest furniture retailer on the East Coast. The one I'm hoping will help me lose the *junior* in front of my title. That presentation." Her thighs turned red and splotchy as she scrubbed them dry. She bent over, flipping her long hair, darkened to the shade of honey from the shower, over Nathan. He shrieked and giggled, trying to grab a handful before she wrapped it up in the towel.

"No, I have an interview at eight thirty. I can't do it."

"You're the boss. You can reschedule the interview. Or just make the guy wait."

"Look, I've already had to reschedule. The guy is driving in from Williamsburg. I'm not rescheduling it again and it's unprofessional to be late. Just have Jenny cover for you till you get there. It'll be fine."

"You promised."

"I didn't promise. I'll see you later. I'm going to be late tonight. I've got dinner with the Macon firm," he said, as he took a step into the bathroom and kissed her on the cheek. "Bye." He gave the baby a pat on the butt and walked out.

"Shit," Billie said into the mirror.

"Sit," Nathan echoed.

"No, no, no. Adult word. Don't say that at daycare." She hoisted the baby to her side and went to see what her daughter was crying about, still naked from her shower.

Thirty minutes later Billie was shoving snacks and papers into an assortment of bags for the day. The trees were blooming, but there was still a chill in the air. If she were a better mother, she'd hunt down matching mittens and wrestle them on wriggling fingers. There was simply no time for that minute detail of parenting. Coats tossed on the foyer floor would have to suffice.

She knew the Finway corporation inside and out, from the store formats to the upper management structure. She would miss the meet-and-greet, but if she hurried she could still make the start of the presentation.

"Sophie, can you carry your bag?" Billie ran to the kitchen to grab her travel mug of coffee. She'd stayed up half the night finessing the presentation. Back to the foyer she shouldered the diaper bag, laptop case, and pocketbook, and reached for the baby. *I guess if everything else fails I could move to Tibet and be a Sherpa.*

"Oh my god, did you poop?" She turned the baby around. Brown mush traveled up his shirt. "Nooo," she said as she picked him up by his armpits, stretched out in front of her like a hand grenade that might detonate at any second, smothering the brief thought that maybe she could just toss him out at the Goddard School and run for cover. Fifteen diaper wipes and another outfit later and they were finally out the door.

The stop-and-go traffic of the lights along Midlothian Turnpike was screwing with her nerves. When she sped up for fifteen seconds, her hopes of making the meeting on time escalated. When she applied brakes, her hopes fell heavy and thick like the yellow tree pollen that covered all the cars.

"Mommy?"

Billie looked in her minivan's rearview mirror at Sophie in her booster seat. Nathan was reaching over from his car seat trying to touch his big sister.

"Yes, baby?"

"You coming to the spring party?"

"No, honey. Mommy's got to work."

"Megan's mommy comes to all the parties." Sophie reached out and slapped at Nathan's hand. He chuckled.

That's because Megan's mommy has nothing better to do, she thought. Billie sighed and reached for her coffee. If she didn't

make this presentation, maybe she'd get fired and be able to go
to all the preschool parties. Start baking cakes, knitting scarves,
and crap like that all day. She took a long look at her daughter
in the rearview, then glanced back at the car in front, which was
way too close with its brake lights on.

"Shit!" She slammed the brakes and skidded to a stop just in
time to avoid rear-ending the guy, spilling her coffee on her shirt.

"Mommy!" shrieked Sophie, accentuated by a *thunk*.

"What the…oh my god!" Nathan's car seat was now facedown
on the floorboard. The light turned to green and a car honked.
Billie turned into the next parking lot. Nathan looked a little
dazed but wasn't bleeding. *Thank god*. He wasn't even crying.

Michael, she thought. He must have just thrown the car seat
in her van the other day after he'd used it. She kissed Nathan
on the head and chewed back tears as she strapped the seatbelt
through the back of his seat. She could not lose it today. She had
to be fresh, even if she was the worst mother in the universe.
Sophie started crying.

"It's okay, honey. Nathan's okay. He's not hurt at all."

"I don't care about that. I want you to come to the party."

"Let's play the quiet game."

The ringing of her cell made Billie jump. It was her assistant,
Jenny.

"I'm sorry, Billie, but Mr. Rollins wants your computer pass-
word so we can get the presentation and start without you."

By the time she entered the conference room, the other junior
account rep had the Finway group laughing, Mr. Rollins nodding,
and Jenny cringing out a sympathetic smile for Billie. Mr. Rollins
told her it was a great presentation, but Max was the one he patted

on the back and asked to go to lunch with him and Mr. Walcott.

It had been a long day.

Friggin' Max, she thought and slammed the bag of frozen gnocchi on the kitchen counter.

She wasn't even sure why she cared so much, besides the injustice of it all. She had gotten into the business because she wanted to design furniture, not try to sell it. Now look at her, sitting behind a computer all day staring at PowerPoint and punching numbers, dressed in skirts and kissing client ass over and over.

Work was bad enough, but when she had picked the kids up from daycare and saw their tired faces under crafted bunny hats, she had the nagging suspicion she was missing out on their lives for nothing. There were lots of hours in the day, and she got... what? Two hours between daycare pickup and bedtime, crammed with dinner, dishes, baths, and tucking in. Billie poured a glass of red wine from a bottle already opened beside a stack of bills. She rolled her sleeves up to tackle the breakfast dishes left in the sink, said a silent prayer that the kids' show wouldn't end before she could get dinner on the table.

Billie jerked awake. Her feet were hanging off the end of the toddler bed. Her arm was numb where Sophie's head rested on it. A Barbie doll dug into her back. Rubbing her eyes, she stumbled, blinkingly, into their bedroom where Michael was removing his shirt and tie.

"Hey. Sorry I'm home so late. I didn't think the Macon guys would ever leave."

Billie shrugged and sat on the edge of their bed.

"Did you pick up the dry cleaning?" he asked as he went into their walk-in closet.

"No. I kind of had a bad day." She turned off the bedside lamp and eased under the covers.

"Dammit, Billie. I ask you to do one thing for me. How could you forget?"

"I don't know, Michael. I guess I'm just as bad a wife as a salesperson," she said.

Michael snorted. "Stop being so dramatic. It was just a presentation."

"Yeah, just a presentation. How did the interview go?"

"Oh, the guy was a complete loser. He showed up twenty minutes late for an interview." Michael came over and slid into his side of the bed. "Do you want to have sex?" he asked against her back.

"Not really," she mumbled.

He slid his arm over her rib cage and cupped her breast. All the things she needed to do hung in her mind. *Hose down the patio and bleach out the cushions on the Adirondacks. Pull the weeds in the flower beds. Sweep the walkway.* His tongue probed the emptiness of her mouth. *Dust the foyer. Shake out the rug. Scrub the kitchen sink.* His weight added to her heaviness. *Mop the floor. Clean closets. Wipe countertops.* His breath came heavy against her neck. *Sweep, dust, mop, fuck, polish, cook, rake, strip the bed, and wash the sheets.* He rolled over, said, "Good night." *And, of course, pick up the dry cleaning.*

HOW MY DAY WENT

He opens the door, takes off his jacket, and gives me that look. The one that asks, *Why is the house still a mess? Why isn't dinner ready?*

Instead he says, "What have you done all day?"

I've: gotten the kids out of bed, scrambled eggs and poured milk, let the dogs out, made pb&j sandwiches to put in plastic, let the kids help even though it would have been quicker if I did it myself, reminded them to brush their teeth, cleared the breakfast dishes, been saddened by the morning news, braided hair, mediated an argument, picked out clothes, nagged that they are going to miss the bus, yelled to go brush their teeth, tied shoes, found jackets, walked to the bus stop, told them to have a good day, hauled dirty laundry downstairs, unloaded the dishwasher, wiped down the table, loaded the dishwasher, scrubbed stains from shirts, thought about calling my mother before it's too late, let the dogs in, put laundry in the washer, sent an email about a PTA fundraiser, counseled a friend having marital issues, volunteered at the school library shelving books in order, put the clothes in the dryer before they mildewed, wiped piss off the bathroom floor, forgotten to eat lunch, tripped over an abandoned baby doll, tried to remember a conversation from 1982, cleaned up dog puke, ran to the store for miscellaneous items you needed, joked with the cashier to make her day easier, ran into a friend who wanted to do lunch sometime—I think she's having marital problems, put my tennis shoes on and ran around the neighborhood because according to you a woman my age has to exercise an hour a day just to stay the same weight, gave the dogs a treat, folded laundry and carried it upstairs, taken a shower, shoved my skinny jeans aside, answered eleven emails about the fundraiser, considered getting a job with a paycheck, petted the dogs so they would know they are loved, walked to the bus stop, gave our children hugs, gave them a snack, reminded them to wash their hands first, shuffled through school papers, encouraged them to learn from their mistakes, signed up to bring in cookies for a class party as soon as I got the note so the teacher would know I appreciated her, sorted through the mail, swept under the table, screened calls from telemarketers, picked up socks, shoes, jackets, and backpacks forgotten in the foyer, listened to our children, reminded them to do their homework, updated Facebook with something cute our children said so I would never forget, yelled turn off the TV, been ignored, taken the trash out, and, just now, sat down with that book I've been wanting to read for three months.

"Nothing important." I get up to start dinner.

LAUNDRY

There's laundry on the elevator walls. Not hanging up, like left to dry on a clothesline, only slick images playing out over cool acrylic. A mantel clock clicks on a rickety table in front of a panel of buttons, mockingly engraved in golden formal script like an invitation.

The buttons lie. She may press *Snowy Day–1998* expecting sledding hills. Instead, images of hands throwing cardigans and wool socks in a dryer flow down on all sides. A familiar voice pleads, as if he's just outside the elevator doors, "Come see our snowman!" The hands add a red scarf to the dryer. She's not sure how long she's been stuck. The clock doesn't work either. It's going backwards.

She eyes *Party–1982* and hesitates, then chooses. Hands ironing flood the walls. She holds up her left hand to the one labeled *1982*. The age spots are gone, yet the bird-shaped scar is still there smoothing a frilly yellow dress. A girl's voice makes her jump. "Come help me frost the cake!" But the slick hands ignore her, pressing out the wrinkles.

A glance at the clock, its tiny black hands edge backwards toward three, dragging slower than feet. She tries to pry open the doors, fists beating like a heart in a chest. There's no emergency call button, no stop. She'll have to choose from what she's got. *Kindergarten–1974* seems as good as any other. *Please let me be doing something, anything, other than laundry.* A curly head rushes past. She clutches at the illusion, wanting to be buried in messy childhood. Snuff out the cloyingly sweet smell of fabric softener permeating the elevator, nesting in her heart. Only her hands just fly off the image of her own hands scrubbing stains off little white shirts.

The air is too fat to breathe. She stares at the clock. It looks gravely out of place. Its hands dredge on, as if they can hardly bear to go around again. She is drowning in a coffin of laundry. Then abruptly the images stop. Blank walls engulf her like a mirror.

STUCK ON YOU

You can't stop thinking that you may be dragging your daughter's body down the street. You didn't see her walk in the building. You're sure she must have walked in the school, but you didn't actually see her go inside. You saw the back of her head disappear out the van door, and then the music teacher waved to you from farther up the sidewalk and you waved back. The door slid shut and you started driving slowly off through the parking lot. You're sure she made it into the school, but what if her backpack got caught in the van door? That ridiculously large princess bag with so many unnecessary straps. Did she trip over one of those straps, get one hung up in the door? The car behind you would notice and honk. You look in the rearview mirror. You know you are being silly, but you can't stop thinking she might be snagged on the car.

It's possible. Freak accidents happen. There was that woman in Connecticut who accidentally ran over her child. The girl was only eight years old, playing hide-and-seek in a leaf pile in the driveway. You couldn't really blame the mother. Who would think a person might be in a pile of leaves? You couldn't blame the girl, either. Of course, the mother probably should have known where her child was before driving away.

And, there was the high school teacher who'd bought doughnuts for her coworkers. She seemed like such a nice lady buying doughnuts for her coworkers, but she'd been in too big a rush, gotten out of routine. She'd forgotten her baby in her seat, left her strapped in the car. It got over a hundred that day. You remember the news anchor said when it's a hundred degrees the inside temperature of a car will reach one hundred fifty in fifteen minutes. The mother forgot her baby for six hours. The baby died. People make careless mistakes.

You would never be so careless. You have not mistaken your daughter for a pile of leaves or forgotten her asleep in the back-seat. Your daughter has not gotten hung up on the car door. If she had, one of the ladies at the drop-off line would have noticed and screamed and waved her arms. You would have noticed the screaming and waving of arms. Unless you were too busy craning your neck, trying to spot your daughter walking in the building—which you did not see. What if you are dragging her and she's still alive? She might still be alive. You haven't gone that far.

You are not going to pull over to check. This is just like last week when you pulled in the church parking lot and walked around your car. Your perfectly normal, reasonable car that was not dragging a little girl's body behind it.

You look in your side-view mirrors. If something happened to your daughter, you wouldn't know what to do. When she was born you were so scared. You'd read the books with chapters on diaper rash and breast-feeding. Books that didn't explain the panic, the complete animalistic fear that you gave birth to alongside your daughter, like a twin. Your husband tried to convince you to have another child a few years back, but you told him worrying about one was a full-time job. Your job. Exhausting. You would rather die than hurt her, any child. You can't understand how any mother could hurt a child. How you could live with yourself if that happened.

You sit up taller behind the steering wheel, look in the rearview mirror again. Turn and look over your shoulder out the back window. Nothing there. By now, it would be too late. She would be a bloody mess, unrecognizable even to you, her mother. It would be on the news, one of those stories that everybody talks about the next day over coffee and exclaims in low, shocked voices, "Can you believe that? How could somebody, *a mother*, be so careless?"

You turn back around to look out the front windshield. The stoplight is red and a girl on a bike is large in front of you. You slam on the brakes, but it is too late. Twisting metal screams and black marks stain pavement. A fragile wheel spins out of control.

JUNK MAIL

The chill seemed to hang on his face like a beard. A real beard would suit William just fine on a day like today, whose clear blue sky hid the truth of the thermometer. A blanket of clouds would do him a favor. He cupped his hands together and blew into them.

Where the hell was Herman? It was four thirty-seven, according to the clichéd Timex the boys had gotten him last year for a retirement gift. Herman was six minutes late. Their house sat just over a rise in the road, so William didn't have the luxury of foresight. There was no, *He's three houses down at the Goodmans. I'll run out now and meet him at the box.* There was nothing, and then all at once a pile of mail crammed into the battered mailbox. Lights fell over the top of the hill, followed by the official vehicle, Herman hanging half out.

"You're six minutes late." William tapped stiff fingers against the watch face.

"I'm a mailman, not a pizza delivery guy." A stack of mail stretched out to William. A laminated ad for fifteen percent off Mattress Warehouse lay on top.

"What the hell, Herman. How many times have I told you to throw this junk out at the post office? I don't want it."

"And how many times have I told you I can't do that? I'm not losing my job or going to jail because you don't like junk mail. I'm not your secretary."

"Yeah, yeah. Have a nice day. Try and be on time tomorrow." William walked up the drive, shuffling through more ads. Underneath was a handwritten envelope with his wife's name, Nancy, scrawled in cramped lettering. *Dammit, Felice.* His breath fogged the windowpane in the door to the detached garage as he punched his passcode into the electronic keypad. It was a little warmer inside, but not much. He pushed the door shut, eyeing the metal cage that dominated the space. The coldness of the padlock burned his fingers as he fumbled with the dial, the flimsy steel walls of the cage chattering. He could see the large rubber trash can watching him through the triangular mesh of cage, like a thousand tiny keyholes waiting to be filled. It took him three tries for the combination with his fingers so numbed. Finally, he swung it open. The lid of the trash can squealed in protest at being removed.

"Dammit, Felice," he swore as he ripped open the letter. He had told her years ago not to write to them anymore. Phone calls were fine. But no more letters. William squinted, trying to decipher the cramped swirls on flowered paper. His wife would love the paper. Felice's granddaughter had her baby. A boy. February third. Six pounds. Eight ounces. His name was Anthony. There was a picture. *Damn, did she have to send a picture?* William held it over the yawning trash can, like it was bored with William's debate over whether to keep the photo for Nancy or give it up. He tossed the flowered paper and the photo in the bin along with the other mail and slammed the lid closed quickly.

Only two more days until trash pickup. Wednesday, their standing date to lunch and the library. Where Nancy would huddle down, buried among the stacks. Her current read, *Atlas Shrugged*, turned to page eight hundred sixty-four. Snuggling in the weight of three hundred thirty-seven pages left in that tomb of a book, almost forgetting that a full trash bin sat on a curb. It was his job to remember the page numbers since he wouldn't allow her to check out books. He would count down the time. Flipping through hunting and travel magazines, eyes lingering on glossy spreads of AK-47 rifles and campgrounds at sunset, until he could be assured that an empty trash can waited at the end of the drive. Greedy to be filled back up with the messiness of their life. *A boy. Six pounds. Eight ounces. Anthony.* He would have to tell Nancy.

William clanked shut the cage, snapped the padlock, and secured the garage door closed. He reached in his jacket pocket for his hand sanitizer, squeezed out a dab and rubbed vigorously, before stomping the short distance over cracked cement to the house. His glasses steamed from the heat when he stepped inside, causing a strange fluttering in his chest like a butterfly suffocating behind glass. Nancy hummed to herself in the kitchen, slicing vegetables to stir-fry for dinner. A partially thawed chicken lay on another cutting board, ready to be chopped and thrown into the sizzling pan. He snatched up the cleaver and, sidling up to Nancy, sank it deep in the raw meat. He pressed the heel of his hand along the knife's spine and looked at his wife. *A boy. Six pounds. Anthony is the name.*

She glanced over at him and asked, "Everything all right out there?"

"Sure." He nodded. "Herman's still a stubborn son of a bitch."

Nancy blew out a long sigh and shook her head, a mostly silent admonishment for his language.

Silence, except for the *chop chop chop*.

"I forgot to tell you, Felice called."

She stopped chopping and looked at his face. He was staring at the chicken pieces. "When?"

He slowly sliced another piece of chicken. "Yesterday."

"Yesterday! Why didn't you tell me?"

"I just said, I forgot."

Nancy started chopping again. "Well, what did she say?"

William cleared his throat. "Mary had her baby."

"She did! Oh my gosh! I can't believe I missed her call."

"A boy. Six pounds. Named him Anthony after Felice's father."

"I was here all day."

"I think you were napping."

"Napping?" William kept slicing. Maybe she would let it go.

"I don't nap, William. You would think after forty years you would know that."

He turned to look at her. "Nancy, what does it matter? Mary had her baby. It's a boy. Six pounds. They named him Anthony. That's it. That's the news. Let it go." He scraped the meat into the pan with the knife.

"No. No, I won't let it go. She sent me a *letter*, didn't she? Where is it? You threw it out, didn't you? How could you?"

"I didn't want to set you off." William wanted to wash his hands, but she was standing in his way.

"You didn't want to set me off? You said I could have a room. One room, remember? Now I'm not even allowed letters—my *real* mail? What other treasures have you thrown away without telling me?"

"Nancy, I can't live that way again."

"You gave me a room!"

He grabbed a wooden spoon from a drawer and stirred the chicken, oil spitting at him from the hot pan. When a man retired after so many years and reentered the home, resentment was bound to leak out of corners and seep from under the beds where it had been lingering for the past forty years, gathering and stacking up, waiting for its opportunity to smother you. He'd been warned by a few of his former coworkers those last couple weeks. They'd stopped by to take him to lunch on the pretense of celebrating, then slipped advice for staying busy and out of the missus's hair into the conversation before the check came.

"Let's just finish cooking and eat. Okay?"

The rest of the evening they communicated through a series of complicated non-gestures, the slamming of drawers and pots used as punctuation. William wouldn't remember what the stir-fry tasted like, but at the time bitterness coated the meal like a condiment poured by a heavy hand. He just wanted to go to sleep.

As he was getting into bed, something snagged his pajama pant leg lightly, but scratched hard at his mind as he lay there. *What was that? It's nothing. Just go to sleep.* He flung the covers back, heaved himself out of bed, and pulled up the fitted sheet. A red cardboard corner peeked out of a slit in the seam of the mattress—a flattened cereal box. He pulled out more: cellophane-windowed envelopes, renewals for magazine subscriptions long gone, and a card claiming they had won a beach vacation for two.

William looked at his wife's back, her face turned toward the wall, and took aim. The mail went sailing off in different directions, wafting down to the floor. The cereal box ricocheted off her left shoulder. She sat up, rubbing it.

"What the hell, Nancy!"

"It's just a couple of things, William," she screamed. She jumped out of bed faster than he had seen her move in twenty years, scrambling for the junk. "You said I could have a room!"

"Then put it in your room," he yelled. He grabbed her by her upper arm and dragged her down the hall to a closed door, the last one. "Go ahead, put it in your room," he shouted, trying to shoulder the door open. "Look at this, will ya? This room's storing all your crazy, and *it's all full up!*" He snatched the cereal box from her and bent down, trying to force it underneath the door. "You can't cram any more shit in there!" William started laughing. "We're all full up, Nancy! I'm just as crazy as you are for putting up with it for all these years. When do I get free from this? When I'm dead and buried?" Quietly, he said, "I can't live this way anymore." He pushed past her, grabbed his wallet and keys off their bedroom dresser, and left without taking a single thing else.

The hush of the house filled up Nancy and buoyed her on waves to their bedroom. Under abandoned lingerie, in the thin, long drawer of the armoire, she reached for the padlock cutters. They had been waiting. An elbow buffered by a towel broke the glass of the garage door. One snip with applied pressure and she was in the steel cage. She took a deep breath and lifted the lid with a flourish, like it contained a gourmet meal at a five-star restaurant instead of trash in a middle-class garage. Felice's letter sat on top, yearning for Nancy's protection. This was important. The flowered paper was so delicate. And a picture! How could William have withheld this from her? What other treasures had he thrown away so callously? She picked up the fifteen-percent-off Mattress Warehouse coupon. She gasped, clutching it to her chest. She had plenty of empty space that still needed to be filled.

———

ALTAVISTA

Items from the *Gazette*, April 6, 1913:

SHREWSBURY, Ark. —
Our community was deeply shocked
Saturday by the terrible death of Samuel
Matthews. He was stabbed in the heart
by Earnest Hickman with no evident
provocation.

Master Davis Dehart had the misad-
venture of falling and breaking his arm.
He was escorted to Fayetteville Hospital
where he is recuperating.

Misses Hazel and Grace Anderson of
Compton were guests of Misses Nellie
and Ada Brown Saturday and Sunday.

Dr. J.W. Witherspoon spent the day
Saturday in Valley Springs.

Headmaster Everett Edwards visited
Altavista Saturday.

Everett Edwards was exhausted. It had been a hard drive from
Altavista to Fayetteville, even if he did own a new Model T. He
brushed the dust off his trousers with the brim of his bowler and
shook the weariness from his shoulders before opening the door
to Fayetteville Hospital. Thank god it had been a dry spring, or

he never would have made it.

The nurses at the receiving desk looked up, dark hair in various stages of escape from the stark whiteness of their caps, reminding him of nuns. He clasped the dusty hat to his chest.

"Mistresses." He nodded and asked where he might find Master Davis Dehart.

He entered the room without knocking. The boy tried to straighten up taller in bed, but his bandaged arm gave a painful yank, which he covered with a twisted smile.

"It's okay, dear boy, please sit still. Did you have to get busted up and shipped to the big city?" Edwards searched for a spot on the boy that might warrant a touch, settled for a pat to his leg.

"Yes, sir. I can't believe you came all this way to see me." The boy gulped and stared at Edwards like he might burst into flames at any moment.

"Not visit one of my most promising students who has been injured? Impossible. How are you?"

Davis pulled the gray blanket tight against his chest, resting his hand over his heart. "I slipped." He paused a moment. "It was awful." He looked at the professor.

"How did it go?" Edwards asked softly.

"Mr. Matthews had just given me a peppermint. You know, the ones he keeps in the glass jar beside the register for customers to suck on while he cuts the meat and strings the package?"

Edwards nodded. He did not want to hear what the boy had to say, but he hadn't driven all the way from Altavista to Fayetteville in a day to back out now.

"He was a good man. His wife is a nice lady. She always smiles at me when she's in the shop." The boy nodded, mustering up his courage. "He didn't deserve it."

That's what I'm afraid of, Edwards thought, wiping his brow with the red handkerchief from his coat pocket. "Go on, Davis."

"Well that's when Mr. Hickman came in. I had just popped that peppermint in my mouth when the bell over the door chimed, and in walks Mr. Hickman lookin' red in the face with spit flyin' out of his mouth like flames."

The boy's hand crept up to the edge of the coarse blanket and gripped it tight. "I told the reporters from the papers I couldn't remember what he said…but that's not exactly true."

Edwards' stomach burned. "You can tell me, son."

Davis hesitated, then relief stretched him forward, pulling the words from his chest in a rush. "He said, *I know it was you. I know it was you, you sick bastard.* Excuse me, sir. But that's what he said, and then he…he grabbed the knife out of the brisket Mr. Matthews was slicin' for my ma and shoved it hard into his heart."

Edwards knew he should tell the boy it was okay to stop, but he felt numbed, like he was looking at himself standing beside the boy's hospital bed from a distance, like he had been the one stabbed in the heart and his soul was abandoning his body. "Tell me," he managed to get out.

"There was so much blood. And the funny thing is, I stood there wonderin' which blood was from the brisket and which was from poor old Mr. Matthews."

Edwards patted the boy's leg as he started to cry softly, pulling the blanket against his eyes. It muffled his next words. "Mr. Hickman rushed past me back out the door. I ran around the counter to help Mr. Matthews, but there was so much blood and I slipped and fell and hurt my arm."

Davis sniffed, wiping his nose on the blanket, looking abashedly up at Edwards.

"You did good, boy."

"They say I passed out. Misses Nellie and Ada found me lyin' beside Mr. Matthews with so much blood over us, they thought we were both dead. Dr. Witherspoon said he heard 'em scream all the way in Valley Springs, but I think he was just tryin' to make me feel better about everything."

Edwards wished he could reverse the past twenty-four hours. He would never have gone to Altavista. He would never have done a lot of things. Mere minutes stretched out an eternity and the room began to feel like a coffin. He gave his good-byes.

Edwards breathed in the clean mountain air, now tainted with a faint smell of rusty metal and peppermint he knew was only his imagination. A lady descended the steps of a livery in front of the hospital. He knew who she was before the tip of her hat lifted and heart-shaped lips piqued in surprise at finding him standing there. Her flush brightened green eyes, and he swore under his breath before meeting her on the walkway.

"Mrs. Hickman." He nodded firmly, bringing her hand up for a kiss.

"Everett. So, I'm already back to *Mrs.* instead of Hattie? We're not *that* far away from Altavista."

Edwards raised his eyebrows and smirked. "I thought you'd be in jail visiting Mr. Hickman. Remember him?"

If he didn't know better, he would have sworn she blinked away tears before placing her hand on his lapel and, leaning in, said, "I did an awful thing."

"More awful than the other things you've been doing?" he whispered in her ear.

She lowered her gaze to her patent leather pumps, too fancy

for a carpenter's wife. "What did you do, Hattie?"

"He wanted a name. After I got back from Altavista, he demanded I tell him a name."

"You didn't."

"Would you have rather I said yours?"

Edwards looked at the wheel of his Model T, scuffed and dirty from the furious drive. He shook his head.

Her glare cut as she walked past him toward the hospital. "I didn't think so," stabbed into him as she opened the door and let it shut firmly behind her.

TIGHTER

Helen Matthews clutched her sister Minnie's forearms and hoisted her into the back of the kid hack, as she had done every day of school for as long as she could remember. A pang stitched her side. She gathered her skirts and sat on the bench seat that ran the length of the vehicle. Minnie fell jerkily into place beside her. The other children continued their teasing and swatting at flies without looking at the sisters. Their jeers had dissipated through the years, but Helen knew their scorn still clung to them like dirt from their parents' farms. She would rather walk to school like the rest of the town kids, but the five short blocks might as well have been a hundred for Minnie.

Rebecca Highman leaned over Minnie, aimed a smirk at Helen. "Anne Whithers got a letter from Tommy. Looks like he's finished basic and startin' his pilot schooling." She raised her stenciled eyebrows high. "You heard from him lately?"

Helen rolled the closest window's canvas flap up. The stench of manure and mules mingled with the cloying smells of bodies slick with sunrise chores, but the slight breeze caressed her cheek just the same. "Of course." The hack moved in stiff, awkward bursts as the driver whipped the mules, then alternately reined the harnesses taut to avoid other carriages.

Helen thought about her last three letters that had gone unanswered. She shouldn't have asked Tommy for the dollar.

They made the right turn onto Grace Street and she let the
canvas slap back into place. She didn't want to see those tight
corsets in the Schreier & Son window display, that mannequin
standing, serenely slender-waisted, like there wasn't a care in the
world. She had found herself drawn to the window a foolish
amount of times in the past six months. Ever since Tommy's
boyhood excitement over Ely's takeoff from the USS *Birmingham*
had turned into manly *what-ifs* when the 1914 assassination of
Austria's archduke sparked the Great War. She shouldn't have
let a boy's grand ideals of defending a nation catch hold of her;
she had plenty to defend right here at 53 Full Maple Lane.

She looked at Minnie slouched and squeezing her palms
together, trying to keep her arms quiet. Mama's clockwork assault,
over eggs and toast, to send Minnie to the State School for the
Feeble-Minded had triggered Helen's refrain, "Her mind's clear.
She has Little's Disease is all." Helen smoothed the fabric of her
dress, her mama's words banging in her head, "Why couldn't
God have just made her deaf and dumb? They got schools for
mutes." She pushed down on a swell in the fabric. She had
mended her corset a half dozen times, but the baleen casing
was now gapped, the two sides left reaching like illicit lovers
denied an embrace. She suspected too much time had passed
for it to be fixed.

In twenty-eight days she'd be a graduate of Norfolk High
School. She needed that diploma. She couldn't leave Minnie to
Mama. She couldn't leave much to Mama. She would concoct
one of her home remedies to take care of it, turpentine and
pennyroyal stinking up the house. How many times had Aunt
Hazel whispered over tea that her mama's home remedies were
the root of Hazel's own poor constitution and, of course, Minnie.

If only Tommy hadn't gotten stationed in Charleston. Two years later he could have stayed in town, when 474 acres were purchased and construction started with purpose on the Norfolk naval base. The land that was now just a pretty spot to go fishing or whisper *what-ifs*, watch the sun's fading reflected. Tommy's first letters had come frequently with wild descriptions of the Cooper River at sunset and how it reminded him of home and the flow of her hair. His letters had dulled, eventually dried up, like they'd been left out in the sun too long.

Tommy wasn't going to save her. He was too occupied saving the country. She had to get that diploma, and the corset was the only way. She had scrimped, gone without even fifteen-cent meals, and hid some of her sewing money from Mama. She had the dollar price for the corset in her pocketbook, and after she deposited Minnie in her training class she was feigning womanly ills. Only a certain silhouette would guarantee graduation, which in turn would help secure a salesclerk position at six dollars a week. She prayed it would be enough for room and board for Minnie and herself, and whatever came along. Thank goodness Preacher Watkins clamored against tightlacing from the pulpit with the fervor of a sergeant commanding his regiment, and waistlines were gradually expanding throughout the city. Helen had given up on God rescuing her from her predicament, but fashion trends and the Rational Dress Society's battle cries to "Emancipate the waist!" still might.

The Great War died with a piece of paper in a mirrored hall, five years to the day it was consummated. The world's labor pains birthed American women's right to vote, although it would take half a century more before they won equal education and pay.

Helen received her own hard-won piece of paper while whispers about her shape spread through the aisles of capped classmates, like a rain-swollen river flooding its banks.

Ten million military men were killed in the war; one of them was Tommy. He never got a chance to fly in and save her, and she had long since rationed the energy for wishes into working nine-hour days at the five-and-dime, fighting for Minnie to go to school, and playing "Bring Back My Daddy to Me" on the landlord's Victrola, until he told her he'd rather hear crying than that song one more time.

KING OF THE HEAP

My name is Maxwell Anderson. My friends call me Max. Leo Williams is my best friend. He lives down the street, a couple blocks closer to the stack, which gives him an unfair advantage. When I told him that's why he's won the past three days, he just grinned and yelled, "King of the Heap!" then shoved me off the stack. I plan on winning today.

Aunt Clara's hawk eyes caught me at the front door and I had to stand in the dining room while Ma hung camphor balls around my neck and made me put two sugar cubes burnin' of kerosene under my tongue. One thing's for sure, I stink to high heaven. There goes my sneak attack on Leo. Thanks to Aunt Clara. When she came to live with us she brought three things to decorate our house: a photo of Uncle Robert dead in his casket, a permanent frown under hawk eyes, and a vase of peacock feathers which Leo told me was bad luck but Ma says looks pretty and makes Aunt Clara happy. How she knows that I have no idea. The only time I've ever seen Aunt Clara's mouth move into any semblance of a smile was when she was quoting Billy Sunday about praying down sin to get rid of sickness. At least Uncle Robert died with honors, buried in his navy blues.

I bang the front door behind me, cutting off Ma's warning to, "Stay off those caskets, there's sick peo—" and I'm off running down the street. My baby sister, Evie, is jumping rope with her little friend Harriett, and I stop to give a pull on both pigtails and a pinch on her nose. I don't pull too hard and she smiles at me but keeps on singing and twirling the rope for Harriett, the other end tied to a fence post. "I had a little bird. Its name was Enza. I opened the window, and in flew Enza."

I run past the Johnstons' house. There's a gray crepe on the front door, and I wonder if Mr. or Mrs. Johnston is the one that died. My money's on Mr. Johnston. He was always too pale looking and bunched up like a frightened chick when the missus hollered at him to come in for supper. Could go either way though, they were both older than Christmas. I wished I had time to run down Edwards Street to see the crepes there. Maybe Leo has the news.

Leo's always bragging about how his pa got picked to lead an army combat troop overseas. I guess he doesn't stop to think how I feel stuck with a pa with a bum leg still in town. My pa got chosen health officer for Blithesville, which just means he sits at his desk and looks worried. He posted, THIS TOWN IS QUARANTINED. DO NOT STOP, on the population sign on Main Street, but I guess the flu can't read, or doesn't mind nobody's signs, because it came anyways.

Leo said yesterday that there'd been a telegraph from his pa saying he was coming home. He's all excited to see his pa since he's been gone since Leo's last birthday when he turned ten, and his next birthday's only a few weeks away. I tried to act excited for Leo, and I guess I was a little bit, but it's kind of hard to be excited about a pa coming home when yours never left. Leo said his ma looked bluish when she read the telegram, but I didn't ask if he meant sad or sick. I overheard Aunt Clara and Pa talking about how near the end the sick turn black and blue like storm clouds and rain red out their ears and eyes and mouth. Ma said, "Keep your words to yourself," to Pa when I woke up with nightmares. I was sorry I got him in trouble, but I couldn't help it.

I trip to a stop in front of Leo's house, skin my knee. There's a black crepe on his door. That means he meant sick blue. I look at the cracked sidewalk I tripped on and finally find my excitement about his pa coming back. I walk slower now, running my hand along the fence slats, toward the stack. The street is empty except for the open truck stopped in front of the stack, adding five more boxes to the pyramid. The worker's masked face turns to take me in and then shoves the pine box firmly on top.

Mr. Wallace, the undertaker, steps outside to give instructions to the man to add the rest to the base so it doesn't topple over. He sees me and spits out under his breath, "Don't know why they call it the Spanish flu when it's those goddamn Germans that grew those germs," like I'm a man, and goes back inside. Through the glass pane I watch him counting caskets. He must lose count 'cause he slams his palm against pine and goes back to where he started and starts again. The masked man is already driving down the street, looking for more boxes on porches to collect.

The stack is larger than ever, and I stand and admire it for a minute but don't bother climbing to the top. Without Leo here, I guess I'm King of the Heap, but it doesn't feel like a victory. It feels like loss.

I want to see my friend and tell him the news, even if his ma is dead. When I get to his gate I glance up the walk, consider knocking on his door. A white crepe hangs beside the black one for his Ma. It stands there like a ghost sneaking out of the shadows and I stare with eyes frozen. My heart refuses to beat, until the air rushes out of my lungs with a whoosh, pushing me along toward my home. I start to run and get flattened by a broad chest in drab olive, a suitcase knocked to the ground. Leo's pa catches me by one arm and says something I can't hear over the blood roaring in my ears. He gives me a little shake and my gaze travels from his nose to the splatter of blood on my arm. He follows my gaze and lets me go.

My legs pump hard as I run past the Whitmans' black crepe, and the white one next to them at the Hicksons'. So many more crepes since yesterday. It's like the crepes are contagion themselves. Could there be one on my door waiting for my arrival to spread its message—white for Evie, black for Ma or Pa? I see the front gate, our door is empty. I run up the path and swing the door open, glad to find Pa at his desk, signing death notices.

LAST CHANCE NIGHTCLUB

They've started up with that song again. The world's gone mad with joy. Laughter like sniper bullets flash through any crowd, rapid-fire catching. The men transformed, little boys in church secret-code grinning and bursting to get out of their uniforms. Caught singing snippets.

It's strange to be standing here snapping shots of happy faces. I can't sleep, so I watch the dance halls fill and empty. It's like this every night since the news. Their dancing feet stomp on planks, reminding me of the thud of grenades. I anticipate more than laughter.

Russian accents blend with our GIs, but the voices twirl instead of clang. Feet fly frantic like we're beating out flames, not fanning a fire. The smoke is seeping in, though—rising. We are surrounded by gray. Is it wrong to have a pinch of fun, dancing around unmarked graves? Anybody's name could be etched here.

Things rumored to be true—are. I've sent piles of dry pictures home. Bodies piled up like lumber, staving off the cold days of 1944. SS *Suicide* has docked in Nazi towns. Cyanide-spiked lemonade given to daughters, party guests blown to bits by hosts. I worry that it makes me glad, but the smell of burning climbs barbed wire and hangs in the streets, smothering any compassion I may have felt for party-line followers. We have liberated bodies.

Skeletons are dragged out and fed powdered milk until they can find their humanity again.

I'm searching for humanity, too. We all are. That's why they're dancing and I'm filling every frame with strong arms holding on to swirling smiles, tight like the world might depend on it. Don't stop the world—we need it slightly out of focus.

That's why they've started up that song again. A peppy tune to rebuild bloodied rubble. And, that's why we're here. We are the bugle boys playing "Reveille." Shouting out the cry for the world to wake up. I cannot sleep. I will never sleep again. It's the spring of 1945, and we are all awake.

NIGHT SCHOOL SHOWDOWN

First night of writing class, a half dozen of us are
corralled at a table. The usual bandits. Mary Jo.
Her five kids in college now. Done with her and
homeschooling. Gave her this class as a gift. Said,
Skedaddle! Get out of town. Mr. Brooks. A retired
accountant. Tired of cooking the books. Says it'll
warm the cockles of his heart to pen a story. Finally
hit pay dirt!

Then the new girl moseys in. Sits catty-cornered to
me. Looking twenty years younger than the room.
Eyes shoot bullets, ricocheting all over the place.
Mary Jo ducks over her journal. Mr. Brooks's pen is
cocked and primed. She's gussied up in lip gloss and
knee-length boots. Kelly, a copywriter gone rogue.
Wants to grab the reins of her art. Tie her cart to the
hitching post of literature. Harness something more
permanent than thirty seconds. Has a thirteen-year-
old stepson.

I hold my horses until the break. Then I lasso her in,
tell her I started out in advertising. Wore a business
suit even though the creative side drew me. Always

thought I'd been happier if I'd aimed straight and narrow from the get-go. Got a gig designing graphics or writing copy like her. Instead of shooting out instructions with deadlines. Have a thirteen-year-old son, too.

Raised my hackles to see her sitting there. Counterfeit me. My alternate version still—still ending up in the Weinstein Room at the art center. Then I thought, all twenty-year-old bets are made against a stacked deck. Greenhorns cheating themselves instead of the dealer. That forty isn't a bad age to knock the dust off my keyboard. Head over the hill. Write off in to the sunset. Holster regret.

LIGHTER

The lady in blue settles into the faded cushion of her front-row seat. The lights shining on the stage curtain cause her white hair to appear silver. She turns to the young woman seated beside her, a stranger.

Have you ever seen *Giselle*? Oh, then this will be a real treat for you. This prima ballerina is one of the best in the world. Her lines are spectacular. She reminds me of myself many years ago. You know, I was prima ballerina once with City Ballet, too.

The older lady gazes up, traces curlicues of gold sewn along the curtain's edge.

Of course, she's getting old.

The old lady laughs.

You must think it's strange for an old woman like me to talk of someone twenty-seven as old. You must be about that age? I probably look a hundred years old to you. Sometimes I feel a hundred. And sometimes I still feel nineteen. That's odd, isn't it? How you can feel such contradictory things almost at the same time. Like all the selves you've ever been store up inside you and fight for territory. Draw lines down the bedroom of your brain like siblings quarreling.

I haven't seen *Giselle* in a long time. You know the name Giselle means pledge or hostage. My first starring role with City Ballet was as Giselle. Of course, I'd had many, many roles before that one. But this was the dance that changed everything. This was the role that meant our move to New York City had finally paid off. It was a huge honor for me, and Richard loved me enough to act like he was glad. The ballet and Richard, that was all I wanted.

You look like you can understand. You look like you just came from the office. That's a lovely charcoal-gray suit. The color makes the blue of your eyes sparkle. I'm sure a pretty girl like you has a nice fella. A good job and a nice fella, sounds perfect, doesn't it?

The old lady skims through her theater program absentmindedly.

When we first got to the city, we were living off Richard's teacher's salary and couldn't afford more than a third-floor walk-up above an Irish pub, but it felt like each step was another one closer to our dreams. I was too young or stubborn to realize dreams needed to be prioritized. The goal couldn't just be getting to the top empty-handed.

I was happy to stop on the third floor, after dancing nine-hour days. Chinese takeout and a bottle of Heineken seemed extravagant and worldly. Richard needed more, more steps.

Maybe that's my one complaint about the ballet, women lean on men too much. They get lifted, carried, held. I'm not so sure that's the truth. Seems like any time something heavy came along with Richard and me, I did all the lifting and carrying—the holding up.

The old lady looks toward the stage blankly.

That's not true either. Maybe he just knew earlier than I did that choices aren't limitless. You can't hold everything together for long without having to choose something to put down. Nowadays girls do it all the time, but back then, I'm ashamed to say, it wasn't even legal. Afterwards, you'd have thought I'd have felt lighter, but I grew too heavy to make it up those three short flights. I stayed in the studio, danced when I didn't have to sleep or eat.

Richard didn't understand. To be fair, I don't really think anyone can understand unless you're a dancer, or maybe an artist. How you can lose yourself and find yourself all at the same instant, a spiral up and down, like every second of your life from birth to death is contained in that string of pirouettes across the stage. You've found your reason in life. It is glorious, and in the end the entire world stands up and thunders their approval of any sacrifices you have given for that moment.

The heavy curtain opens and glittery lights illuminate the dancers on stage. The women stare at them. The dancers cast shadows that move across the old woman's face.

Shhh. It's about to start.

ACKNOWLEDGMENTS

My beta readers gave invaluable feedback on *The Strangeness of Men*. Their comments were vital to the final ordering of stories and taught me that sometimes *clearer* is better than *clever*. For these reasons and more, I thank Anita Crean, Jennifer Poulin James, Jennifer Leon, Shannon Breazeale Lindsay, Lori Loomis, Jay Reddick, and Brad Tate. Brad, I'll think about adding fighting apes to the next book.

Bookfly Design's James T. Egan worked magic on the cover. Kira Rubenthaler's editing skills and gracious responses to my endless questions were a lifesaver.

Three years ago, after more than a decade of toying with novel writing, I signed up for a community college writing course with Kelsey Trom. She believed in me more than I did myself and represents all that a teacher should be. I'm thankful for all the teachers who share their talents at local art centers with those either less fortunate to have found their passions early in life or who are unable to attend full-time university. I've taken many a creative writing class at the Virginia Museum of Fine Arts and the Visual Arts Center in Richmond. Several of the stories in this collection originated in those classrooms.

I'm proud to be a part of organizations that tirelessly promote literary arts in their community—James River Writers and Poetry Virginia. Writers need other writers. For years my fiction critique group encouraged and prodded each other to keep writing. Anita, Nancy, Stephanie, Ted, and I spent many Sundays splitting cookies and fixing narratives. Linda, Karen, Rita, Julie, Judy, and Joanna are currently helping me become a better poet. I've been blessed to be a part of several fabulous book clubs through the years that not only shared a love of reading and wine, but also occasionally gave me feedback on novels now stashed in drawers.

I'd like to thank the editors that take chances on debut writers, publishing fresh stories and faces in their journals. Editors like David Fraser, Jen Falkner, Rebeca Morales, and Robin Stratton accepted my stories and motivated me to keep pursuing my goals. They showed me yet another link in the writing community.

I am touched every time a reader takes the time to send me a note. It quiets that voice that nags, *Why are you doing this with your life?* The late Holly Gilliatt demonstrated faith and perseverance in her writing and gave me the courage to focus on the next level of my process.

I'd be remiss if I did not thank my family, who has suffered with me on this publishing journey—always welcoming me back to the dinner table. My parents and sisters for listening when I read my tales, laughing at the right spots. My nieces for clutching themselves in terror at my poor excuses for late-night ghost stories. My father-in-law for dealing with the internet to read my newsletters. My husband, Wen, for loving me at my craziest. And, especially to my children, who remind me that our possibilities never dry up if we have motivation and wonder. Ian, Kaelin, and Elliott—you're more important than all the books in the world, but even so, I love when you tell me a good story.

CPSIA information can be obtained
at www.ICGtesting.com
Printed in the USA
FFOW04n0322090715
14829FF